A
homestead
holiday

a prairie creek romance

ELIZABETH
BROMKE

Prologue

When Molly was just a girl, her mimi stood beside her at the family's old oak kitchen table and slung a threadbare dishtowel over one shoulder.

Bowls and spoons were laid neatly in a row in front of them. Behind those, jutted out tins of powders and spices in various heights like a little culinary skyline. A bowl of farm fresh eggs stood at attention on the left. On the right side sagged a stick of salted butter.

Molly had felt like they were about to concoct a potion. Instead, it was her first lesson in cooking and baking. Or, as Mimi called it: *cuisine*.

Molly, mon amour, the old woman had said, *before we begin, there are three truths you must know about cuisine.*

Little Molly had nodded along, wide-eyed and enchanted with the French woman's exotic accent and her watery blue eyes.

Une, a clean kitchen. You begin with a clean kitchen, and

your food is safe. Mimi had waved her hand like a wand across their impeccably scrubbed surface.

Again, Molly had nodded.

Deux, wholesome ingredients. You use wholesome ingredients, and your food is good. Mimi had patted the eggs gently.

Molly had already known this one. Her mom had always been a stickler about eating healthy.

And trois, le cœur. Mimi had tapped a crooked finger on her chest.

Molly had scrunched up her nose and cocked her head, shuffling through her brain for the little French she knew.

"Le curr?" Molly had asked. "Color?"

Mimi had laughed. *The* heart, *mon amour. You cook with your heart, and your food is love.*

Chapter 1 — Molly

September fell over Prairie Creek, South Dakota, like flour through a sifter. The long, hot days of summer were a thing of the past.

Sweaters and boots reemerged from hope chests. Parents shopped for school supplies. Teenagers dreaded the return of homework.

At the present moment, Molly Maison stood behind a narrow folding table. Before her, she'd laid out a red-and-white checkered tablecloth. On top of that, two neat stacks of handouts flanked a set of dressed-up platters. Finally, on the platters rested four dozen sugar cookies shaped like apples and frosted over in a deep warm red with green and brown sprigs of color. If this were a competition, Molly felt confident she'd win. After all, she'd used Mimi's recipe for the cookies.

Around her, Prairie Creek High School's gymnasium was alive with bustling teachers and stressed administrators. It was the highly anticipated P.C.H.S. back-to-school night, which Molly came to learn was disguised as a community fall festival. Anything to trick kids to show up, apparently.

Anyway, as such, today parents and students were able to come and get their class schedules, meet their teachers, and sample the extracurriculars. From what Molly could see, even each sports team was represented. For such a small-town school, the excitement brewing implied this was the area's biggest event. Even the cafeteria staff was on hand serving a spaghetti dinner.

Molly made a mental note about coordinating her program with the food services next year. This was the exact sort of opportunity to highlight the culinary program and just how much she had to bring to the table.

So to speak.

Her eyes flicked around nervously as she took stock of her neighboring tables. On her right was the drama club, led by a woman clad in a cheetah print mumu. Students continually swooped back to the table, giddy and chatty, grabbing brochures designed to look like playbills to distribute among the meandering families.

On Molly's left was the science department chair whose main goal seemed to be to track down students who'd never paid lab fees in years past. From what she could tell, it wasn't going well.

"Hi!"

A sweet little voice jerked Molly from her people watching. The voice belonged to a cute redhead with freckles for days. She was smaller than Molly expected of a high school student. But her confidence was probably bigger than the average adult's.

"Hi!" Molly replied, quick to pluck a page from each of

her stacks. She readied them but first indicated the cookies. "Help yourself. I'm Miss Maison."

"You're the new Culinary Arts teacher?"

"That's right!"

"Welcome to Prairie Creek High." She jutted out a hand. "I'm Penny. Penny Caroline Porter, and I want to learn how to cook."

Warmth spread through Molly's whole body. "Penny, I'm just the teacher for you."

She watched in anticipation as the girl enjoyed a cookie and read through the syllabus.

"Any questions?" Molly asked when Penny's eyes lifted from the page, her mouth edged in cookie crumbs.

Before Penny could launch into the inquiry that seemed to be dancing behind her green eyes, another visitor appeared.

Mr. Porter.

Oh, *right*. Penny *Porter*.

Penny wasn't just a bubbly student looking for a new hobby. She was also the principal's daughter. Molly realized this could be very good or very bad.

"Penny, I thought you were taking drama this year?" The tall administrator was dressed up as something of a principal-cowboy mix, complete with a ten-gallon hat, bolo tie, and oiled leather boots. He winked at Molly. "No offense, Ms. Maison." He got her name all wrong. It was French, pronounced like *May-zone*, but Mr. Porter said Maison like a mason jar. In fact, most people did, but his dialect was particularly...lazy. "This here is my youngest, Penelope Porter. She's talked all *summer* about taking drama."

Penny nibbled her cookie more slowly now and avoided Molly's gaze.

Shifting uncomfortably, Molly tried for cheeriness. "Drama is great too!"

Penny shrugged. "I think I want to take Culinary Arts now."

Mr. Porter rolled his eyes with exaggeration. "Kids." He winked at Molly again. "So, how are you liking Prairie Creek, Ms. Maison?"

"I really like it. Everyone's very welcoming. And especially here. And this—this event..." she shook her head and clicked her tongue as if to say, *Wow*.

He grinned and tipped his hat toward her. "I know you met all the staff earlier in the week, but if you want to tag along with me, I can introduce you to some other Creek folk." He chuckled and hitched his belted pants waist up over his full belly. "That's what we call locals."

Penny cringed, but Molly gave her a warm look before responding. "Well, I'd hate to leave my table." What if someone came and swiped all the cookies? Or worse, what if someone had questions about Culinary Arts, and she wasn't there to answer them?

Mr. Porter waved her off. "It'll be fine. Besides, I can't imagine you're getting *too* much action yet." Another wink.

Molly's face fell, but still she followed her boss across the gym floor.

The principal jabbered along information about some local farming family who always participated in the festival. Even so, it was her own setup that consumed Molly's interest. She looked over her shoulder at her table where Penny remained, alone, eyeing a second cookie. Elsewhere around the gym, teenagers and their parents honed in on the athletics table and the robotics table. Maybe no one had noticed the cookies quite yet.

Molly turned around to see they were headed directly across the gym. Her thoughts were stuck back at her station, though. Her cookies. Her handouts. Would Penny Porter ditch drama and sign up for Culinary Arts? Would *others*?

"Ms. Maison, I think you and the Grangers will get along *just* fine." Mr. Porter waved his hand to where they'd landed.

The setup was something out of *Homestead and Hearth*. Burlap covered the table and on top were mason jars dressed up in ribbons and papyrus labels tied just so. Through the dappled glass, Molly detected jams and jellies, honey, and pickled produce of every color.

Next to the jars was a basket lined with cream colored fabric. Piled inside were little paper covered rectangles, each tied up in string. An unwrapped rectangle stood on a small wooden stand outside of the basket as a sample. It was a rough edged bar of soap, speckled and quaint. The neatly handwritten card propped in front read: *Goat's Milk Soap.* Molly didn't have to inhale to know it smelled of oatmeal and vanilla.

Farther down along the table sat a row of three wooden crates. In the first, fresh-picked apples. The second held a thatch of greens. The third spilled over with summer squash. Again, little cardstock labels sprang out of each box—the handwriting neat and feminine. More than likely, the farm belonged to the grandmother of one of the school's students. The whole thing reminded Molly of her own mimi, after all.

Molly was transported by the charming display. She could have stepped right into Mimi's kitchen. Fresh ingredients. Homemade bread. The smell of garlic and thyme...

But then she lifted her gaze.

Molly blinked. The Granger behind the table was no grandmother.

Chapter 2 — Liam

L iam Granger arrived at Prairie Creek High, unloaded the bed of his truck onto a dolly, and followed the signs.

School Fall Festival THIS WAY.

A whole series of them led him from the parking lot to the gymnasium, where he searched the cavernous space for his Aunt Betsy.

Liam didn't know the first thing about canning peaches or handmade soap. Give him a cow to milk or cattle to drive, and he was golden. But *this*?

Yet here he was, helping his aunt hawk her wares. Aunt Betsy was a regular at farmers' markets, so just as soon as she saw the school's call for vendors, she signed right up.

"It'll be good for you," she'd chided Liam when he agreed to help. "Besides, it's important to remind the community that Granger Ranch exists!" Betsy added, poking her finger into his chest.

Plus, Liam needed a day off. His dad was running him

into the ground. Really, Larry Granger should take a day off too. He was running *himself* into the ground.

Liam wheeled his hand truck along the south side, toward Aunt Betsy, who waved him wildly her way.

"Liam!" she hissed, her face panic-stricken as he unloaded the crates of fresh produce. "I forgot the goldarn *candles* back home!"

"I'll go back and get them," he offered. Liam fancied himself more of an errand boy than a shopkeeper.

"No, no. You'll never find them. I'll go. You stay."

Before he could protest, she was gone, and he was left with a metal cashbox and a pretty table. Liam groaned and shifted his weight irritably, taking in the festival landscape for the first time.

To Liam's untrained eye, it looked far more like a school exposition than a fall festival, but who was he to judge? The last time he'd stepped foot in a school was the day he graduated high school.

He plucked an apple from one of the crates and bit into it just as an ambush struck.

Mr. Porter was headed directly his way.

And he wasn't alone.

"Liam!" Principal Porter was Liam's dad's hunting buddy. "I want you to meet our new hire." He stepped aside to reveal an unfamiliar face.

Liam had barely had a chance to take her in when he swallowed the bite he'd taken. "Hi," he managed, irritated and embarrassed at being caught off guard so early in

Betsy's absence. He felt his face turn even redder when he moved his gaze to the young teacher.

"This is Ms. Maison. She's going to teach cooking for us this year."

"Culinary Arts," she squeaked.

Liam licked his lips and lowered the apple awkwardly. After another swallow, he added, "I'm, um, Liam. Liam Granger." He went to offer his hand only to recall the dang apple core, and that's when things got worse. He started to juggle the apple to his other hand to free up his shaking hand but then realized he was getting apple pulp on *both* hands and finally came up with a half wave and two sticky hands. "Sorry. Um. *Hi*." He shrugged helplessly.

"Hi." She waved back. "I'm Molly. Molly Maison."

Molly.

Mr. Porter cleared his throat. "*Ms*. Maison. She's going to teach cooking, you know. In *fact*," he added in singsong, "Molly is a French cook. French American! Like bonjour and oui! Oui oui!" He laughed hard. So hard in fact that he started coughing. "Oh, heck. I need my heart meds. I'll be back shortly." He left, hacking his way out of the gym.

"*Ms*. Maison," Liam quietly corrected, once the annoying administrator was out of earshot.

She looked down. "I'm not a *real* teacher yet, actually." Liam stole the moment to give her face a better look. He didn't detect one lick of makeup. *Miss* Molly Maison's skin was smooth and creamy. Her face wide and open, and her lips full. Molly's eyebrows were furrowed above a thick line of natural dark lashes. Her hair was thick and long, parted down the center, and tied back from her face. The length of it fell in a gentle rope over her shoulder.

French or not, Molly looked every bit the part of a girl from some far-off land—exquisite and exotic and totally out of his league.

Molly looked back up at him. Her chocolate eyes awaited a response.

He fumbled to recall what they were talking about. Teacher. *Real* teacher. She wasn't one. "Oh, you're a substitute or...?"

Her gaze turned sharp. "*No*. I'm finishing my certification right now. I have my teaching degree, but there's a whole other certification process. I'm almost done."

Liam nodded, confused.

"Well. I'd better get back to my table." Molly hooked her thumb over her shoulder.

"Oh, sure. Yeah." He ran his hand up the back of his head.

She turned to go but then turned back again, frowning and eyeing Betsy's goods.

"Oh, I, um—this isn't me. This isn't *mine*."

"Not yours?"

"No, well—" Liam followed Molly's gaze behind him to where the ranch's sign was hung. *Granger Ranch and Farms*. "Right, well. It's my family's, yes. My Aunt Betsy makes extras for expositions and farmers' markets. So, yeah. That's what this is. I work on the ranch." He realized he needed to shut up. "I'm just helping."

"That's nice." Molly plucked an apple from the bushel. "Do you barter?"

Chapter 3 — Molly

M olly had no idea why she offered a cookie up in exchange for an apple. One, she didn't really want an apple. And second, she had no need for this Liam Granger person to visit her table.

Maybe, deep down, her goal was to show Pompous Principal Porter that there *were* people interested in what she was cooking up.

She pretended to tidy her piles of paper and reorganized her cookie platters as Liam popped a cookie in his mouth. From the corner of her eye, she couldn't help but notice that he had a familiar look about him. Maybe it was the tall, broad build and blond hair. The cornflower blue eyes. He could be just about any midwestern farm boy. Straight out of central casting. The only thing that set him at least a smidge apart was the deep cleft in his chin. Maybe the steel cut of his jaw. His full lips. Other than that, though, Liam could be any other local. A tad younger. A tad cuter. But really, he was just another South Dakotan.

Nothing special.

"Culinary Arts, huh?" he asked after running the back of his hand over his mouth.

"Yes. That's the goal anyway. Mr. Porter signed me on as a floating elective teacher. I'll finish my certification, and he'll sort of check in with me each quarter to see how things are going. If it's going well, and I finish my cert—which I *will*—then I'll sign a contract to teach Culinary Arts."

He nodded disinterestedly.

Molly looked past him to see a group coming her way. Potential students?

"Granger!" the tallest one shouted. A dime-store cowboy, all lanky arms and legs.

Liam turned and groaned at the caller and his group. "Not you people." His words said *go away* but his tone said *Yay*. "Did you guys come around to register for Culinary Arts?"

The tallest one threw a curious glance toward Molly. "Oh, yeah. Penny was talking about it. Where'd she go?"

"Penny." Molly rolled her shoulders back. "Penny Porter. She was here. Yes, I think she's switching over from drama." Her nerves buzzed anxiously.

Liam squeezed the tall boy's shoulder. "Ms. Maison, this here is Parker Porter, Penny's brother and an on-again, off-again farm hand at the ranch."

"You're a *teacher* here?" Parker's eyes lit up.

Molly felt herself flush. She had been dreading this. The inevitable attention of raucous teenage boys with a penchant for bothering newbies. Especially teachers. And *especially* young, pretty teachers. Not that Molly fashioned herself a young, pretty teacher, but she wasn't blind.

So far at Prairie Creek High, she counted exactly three

teachers—including herself—who were under the age of fifty. Two of them were men.

"Don't get any ideas," Liam barked. "Don't you have to retake Freshman Math?"

Parker was unfazed. "Yeah, so? I've always wanted to learn how to—"

"Don't even *think* about finishing that sentence." Liam folded his arms over his chest. "Get outta here. And take this pack of hounds with you."

Molly hid her shock behind her hands, but apparently that did more to draw attention to it. When the boys shuffled away, all whispers and snickers, Liam turned on her.

"What?" he asked.

"They're *kids*."

"They're *seniors*."

"They might be my *students*."

"They *were* my ranch hands."

Molly crossed her arms over her chest. "You can't call them hounds."

"I've called 'em worse."

Was he trying to impress her? Or annoy her? Both?

"Well. I hope you enjoyed that cookie. I'd better get back to work." She set her jaw and gave him as steely a look as she could muster.

"*Work*. Right. Sure." He looked around him. "I'll just be on my way, then."

When he went to leave, Molly called after him. "They might have been my only students! So, *thanks* for scaring them off." As soon as the words flew from her lips, she wanted to kick herself. Molly wasn't desperate, so why was she embarrassing herself like that? Her skin felt hot. She pursed her lips and forced herself to hold Liam's gaze once he turned it back on her.

"You still have Penny, right?" A shrug. "Anyhow, you don't want ranch hands kneading dough. *Trust me.*" He winked at her.

And then he turned and crossed the floor.

Chapter 4 — Liam

As soon as he walked away from Molly and her table of cookies, Liam's pulse slowed to within a normal range again. But then his throat decided to close up and a hot feeling spread over his chest. Maybe he was having an allergic reaction to the cookies. What did she put in them, anyway? Poison?

By the time he'd settled back behind the table and hauled his boots up onto a spare crate, it occurred to him that Betsy ought to be back by now.

He checked his wristwatch. It had been at least half an hour since she left. Maybe forty-five minutes. The ranch was a quick ten minutes straight north of town. Assuming she went right there, grabbed her candles, and headed right back, she should have returned twenty minutes ago or so.

Liam wouldn't care too much—it was easy enough to make change for a twenty and bag up apples and jars— except for the fact that every time he looked up, the first thing he saw was Ms. Molly Maison and her Culinary Arts table. Oh, and Penny Porter, who kept blocking his view.

He checked his watch again. And again.

A set of parents appeared and inquired about Granger Ranch and what in the world it had to do with the school. Liam awkwardly explained that it had little to do with the school. That his aunt treated it like a farmers' market, but that the ranch was locally owned and often hired a lot of the boys from the school.

The parents left, more came around. Some old familiar faces. And a rush of teeny bop girls in hot pursuit of a different rush of teeny bop boys.

Liam yawned.

He checked his watch again.

Over an hour now.

A quick glance across the gym revealed that Molly was courting the parents who'd asked about the ranch earlier. *Good for her*. Pfft.

At this rate, he was long since convinced Betsy had played a dirty trick. She knew how much he hated things like this, so she'd set him up, maybe figuring he'd make a friend or two. That he'd actually *talk* to people.

Or, maybe she couldn't find the candles and had set about making a whole new batch. She'd never make it back in time. The event would wind down within the next hour. He checked her cashbox and assessed inventory. She'd sold most of the jars, all of the soap, and some squash and apples. The greens remained because, well *greens? Really, Betsy?*

It was time he gave her a call.

Liam took out his phone to call and scrolled to her phone number.

A voice interrupted him. "Granger!" It boomed.

Liam looked up. "Phil." His thumb hovered over Betsy's contact, ready to tap *CALL*. "You feeling better?"

"Pardon?" he coughed loudly into his fist.

"Your heart meds—"

"Oh, sure—" Phil waved him off. "I wasn't taking any heart meds. I just wanted the pair of you to have a moment."

"The pair of who?"

"You and Ms. Maison!"

Liam snorted. "Why?"

Phil hooked his thumbs through his belt loops and hitched his jeans higher up on his stomach. "Listen, I'm gonna be honest with you, Granger—"

"Can you hold that thought?" Liam's phone was vibrating in his hand. It was Betsy. "I just need to take this call."

"I'll make it quick," Phil assured him, leaning in and proving he wasn't about to hold any thought.

"I really need to take this call." Betsy was about to be sent to Liam's voicemail.

"Call 'em back. It's probably your dad. Am I right? Nagging you to get back and get to work."

Before Liam could defend his dad, Phil had turned around and was gesticulating wildly across the gym floor.

Directly at Molly.

Betsy's call went to voicemail.

Chapter 5 — Molly

Molly had signed up exactly one person for Culinary Arts, Penny Porter, who continued to hang around, munching the cookies. Where Penny put all that sugar and fat was beyond Molly. The girl was the same height and width as a pin. Molly asked her, "Do you know the Grangers?"

"The Grangers? Sure." Penny spoke through a mouthful of crumbles. "Dad and Larry are best friends. And Liam's cool. But Betsy is my favorite."

"Betsy."

"Betsy Granger. You'll love her."

Molly stowed the name, then frowned across the way. Mr. Porter had returned to the Granger Ranch table and was chatting animatedly with Liam. Molly looked away. The crowd was dwindling. It was nearly time to clean up. She had very little to show for her new program. One enrollee and a couple of empty platters of cookies. Penny hadn't eaten *all* the cookies, though. There had been some attention. Some traffic. Parents inquired about what kids would get to cook or bake. Students slipped cookies and promised to think about changing their schedules.

That was the problem, Molly knew. Most students had already requested their electives by September. Schedules were set. Molly wasn't hired until the summer, and even then she was described to the school community not as the new Culinary Arts teacher but as the new *hire*, a vague term meant to keep things on the up-and-up somehow.

Her courses weren't added into the online scheduling software until August, and by then, no one really cared or knew about Molly or what she had to serve.

With school starting next Monday, Molly would end up having classes full—or *half* full, maybe—of newly enrolled students. Kids who didn't know what an elective was, and kids who were given the boot from their other electives for heaven knew what reason.

Except for Penny, of course.

"I'd better clean up." She pulled a pack of wet wipes from her tote and wiped down the platters.

"Oh *no*," Penny groaned.

Molly looked up. Coming toward them were the rapscallions from earlier. The ones Liam Granger had shooed away. There were five in all, and every boy was clad in Wranglers, cowboy boots, and John Deere t-shirts. They each scowled.

"Is everything okay?" Molly asked the evident leader, the tall one who'd given her attitude earlier.

"You took his place!" the boy said, his voice raised and accusatory.

"Whose place?" Molly looked at Penny for help.

Penny shrank. "Oh, right." Her gaze flew across the

gym, and sure enough, Mr. Porter was crossing toward them with Liam Granger hot on his heels.

"Whoa, whoa, whoa now!" Mr. Porter chuckled and hitched his belt just in time for Molly to become truly and utterly confused.

"She took his place," the tall boy repeated, this time to the principal.

Was Molly in trouble?

"She didn't take anybody's place." Mr. Porter was red faced and all but panting. "Ms. Maison, these here boys must have just now learned about our *former* agriculture teacher."

"Agriculture?"

Penny looked at Molly sadly. "We lost our agriculture teacher," Penny whispered. "You replaced him."

"Replaced the agriculture teacher?" Molly pressed a hand to her chest as if to deny the allegations and assert her innocence. "But I'm teaching *Culinary Arts.*"

"Nobody replaced anybody. We lost Rick. We got Ms. Maison. And a whole new class to boot!" Mr. Porter was all but yelling over the bickering amongst the boys.

Beside him, Liam looked at Molly in helpless consternation as if to say *I don't know anything about this.* Then, he frowned. His hand moved anxiously, revealing his phone screen and an incoming call. She watched as he read the screen. Was it something urgent? His face was all furrows and drawn lines. Probably a girlfriend.

"That's why I wanted to get these two together," Mr. Porter added once the small crowd calmed down enough to reason with.

"Which two would that be?" Molly asked, sliding her

gaze away from Liam, whose face was crumpling further. He glanced up, alarm filling his broad features.

"I have to take this—" he started, but Mr. Porter interrupted him.

"No, no. Just a second now. I wanted to form an alliance, you see. We've got our new teacher here, Ms. Maison—gunning for a cooking class or two or three. And then we've got Liam Granger here, representing his daddy's farm."

Where was this going?

"I really have to take this," Liam repeated.

"I don't need help from the ranch or anything," Molly contended.

"I'm just saying let's see what happens." Mr. Porter was about out of breath, and the boys were losing interest. Penny remained quiet.

"I *am* teaching Culinary Arts still, right?" Molly felt the hair that lined the nape of her neck stand on end.

"Oh, sure. *Sure*," Mr. Porter said. "But you've got a long-term substitute's contract."

"What's your point, Phil?" Liam asked brashly, spitting the words rather than saying them. He held the phone up in front of him and was tapping away furiously as he spoke.

His girlfriend was getting mad at him, maybe. He was texting her sweet promises, Molly was sure.

"My point is that it wouldn't hurt if the ag kids took Culinary Arts," Mr. Porter declared finally. "Just in *case*."

"In case of *what*?" Molly asked.

"Oh *no*," Liam whispered, his gaze cast down at his phone.

All eyes turned on the rancher. Molly felt a stab in her

heart for him. His eyes were watering up. His lower lip trembled. His hand shook.

She took a step nearer, nervous to crowd him but aware that there was no other sympathetic party in attendance. Molly dropped her voice low and gentle. "Is everything okay?"

Liam looked up. A single tear spilt from his eye. His voice cracked. "It's my dad."

Mr. Porter boomed. "You mean Larry?"

Molly's breath stilled in her chest. This wasn't her business.

And yet...stranger or not, another human being's heartache was a thing to tend to. "Your dad?"

Liam looked like he was going to be sick. "I have to go."

Chapter 6 — Molly

In the cafeteria kitchen on Ingalls Lane, Molly Maison pushed her grandmother's rolling pin into a thick ball of sugar cookie dough.

Around her, autumn was turning into winter—Mimi's favorite season. Molly's too.

Today's Christmas Classics played from Molly's school issued laptop. Outside, an early season snow had begun to collect in the corners of the building's casement windows.

Molly ran her palms along the wooden handles of her rolling pin, smoothing the heavy mixture and spreading it up the length of a wide stainless steel counter lined with wax paper. Every time she pushed out dough, she imagined her late grandmother's gnarled hands, caked in flour and warm with love. Remembering the woman gave Molly great peace.

The scent of flour and vanilla filled the air with a nimble fragrance that carried the world from one season to the next. That was the power of baking. It transcended seasons. You could whip together poppyseed muffins for

Easter Sunday, then come Fourth of July it was all about cherry pie. Of course, autumn...well, autumn and winter existed solely for the enjoyment of delectable, flavorful sweets. That's not to mention the many varieties of savory breads, either.

Lifting the heavy wooden pin for a moment, Molly reached into her prep bowl, and scooped a small handful of flour. She sprinkled it like rock salt over the honey colored slab and rolled again.

Once the fresh dough laid out in an even rectangle, she moved her cookie cutter into position, beginning at the very center and working outward.

After repeating the process with two more balls of sugary dough, Molly had three dozen Christmas tree shaped sugar cookies ready to pop in the oven.

Before sliding the baking sheets in, she gave each of the thirty-six a quick coat of melted butter for good measure.

Next was icing prep, which meant food coloring. Lots of food coloring. Green, red, white, and brown tubes awaited her, and she set about mixing up the confectioners' sugar and butter, her arms aching from stirring.

It was November now, and though her classes were small and filled mainly with the outcasts from the now defunct agriculture program, Molly felt confident that they'd mastered the basics. It was time to have a little fun with baking.

Besides, baking cookies taught her pupils the basics of measurements and the chemistry behind every fundamental aspect of cooking. Her plan was to return from the weekend and present her class with the surprise cookies. If all went according to plan, even the most malcontent of students would light up like Christmas trees themselves. Who could resist sneaking a little cookie dough, anyway?

And so, Molly had arrived at the school building early, preheated the stove in the cafeteria—she'd already applied for a grant to furnish her *own* culinary kitchen—and started the dough. All with big hopes for a great school week.

At eight o'clock, just half an hour before the first bell rang, the sound of footsteps echoed along the corridor that led to the cafeteria. By now, Molly had learned to expect teachers or other staff to pop in once they smelled her cooking or baking. She whipped out one of her paper dessert plates and readied a trio of cookies for the uninvited guest.

Instead, it was Penny. Buoyant, jubilant Penny. "Can I do the icing?" Penny shrugged off her backpack and hurried to the sink to *scrub in*, as she liked to put it.

"Packing it now!" Molly scooped the remains of red into an icing bag and twisted the top, handing it off to Penny, who sometimes came around early to help.

To outsiders, the girl might look like a teacher's pet, but she was anything but. Hardheaded and pushy, Penny Porter had a bit of her abrasive father in her. Unlike him, however, she had a soft side. A sweetness and honestness that was hard to find in today's teenager. All in all, Molly adored her.

"Did you happen to apply for that competition?" Molly referred to an email that had come her way. It was a youth culinary contest out of Aberdeen.

Penny sighed but kept her hands steady as she traced green boughs around the first golden cookie. "No. It's the same weekend as the Holiday Festival."

Molly's ears perked up. "Holiday Festival?"

"Right." Another big sigh. "I mean, I *love* the Holiday Festival, but like, I'd also *love* to do a baking competition. I mean look at this." She finished her design and indicated it with her hand. Molly examined the clean lines of her frosting work.

"And you'd do well. Is it a matter of transportation? If your parents are comfortable, I could drive you?"

"Oh, no, Miss Maison. The Holiday Festival is, like, *required*."

"Required?" Molly wondered if *she* would be required to go. "So, it's the weekend of Thanksgiving?"

"The Friday after Thanksgiving. Creek folks don't believe in Black Friday. I think that's when the festival started. It's, like, town *lore*. Legend has it that when Black Friday finally made its way up here, locals were, like, *totally* grossed out. It was Ms. Granger who put her foot down and said that the people of Prairie Creek weren't about to spend the first day of the yuletide season shopping for mini Crock-Pots. Not on her watch, anyway."

"Ms. Granger?" Molly was trying hard to keep up as she swept up after Molly with the white frosting bag and added bits of snow to each Christmas tree cookie. "Would that be Liam's—*wife*?"

"Liam? Oh—" Penny snorted. "No. He's like, *way* too into the ranch. Or, he *was*. He was, like, *obsessed*."

"Obsessed," Molly echoed in a whisper. "And so Ms. Granger is his mom?"

"Oh, no." Penny took the back of her hand and whipped her braid over her shoulder and out of her way, then hunched back down to continue frosting as she spoke. "Ms. Granger is Betsy, Liam's aunt. She is, like, the *face* of the ranch. She's everywhere, all the time. She was just here at school this morning!"

"This morning? Here?" Molly frowned. "Why?"

Penny shrugged. "Who knows? She's the *ultimate* busybody. *Anyway*, she, like, started this Holiday Festival thing where their ranch puts up all its harvest for sale for, like, totally cheap. And they have a huge community supper thing in their barn for anyone in need. It's *so* legit."

"Legit?" Molly repeated again. "Right." She thought for a moment. "Isn't it cold, though? For that sort of thing? A ranch setting?"

"It's literally *freezing*. But they open up the barn and this other huge building. Plus, they put up massive heater things and there's a huge bonfire. They give out hot cocoa, for *free*."

"Why do they do this? How does the ranch make any money?" Molly was sucked into the gossip—was it gossip? The business of the Granger Ranch.

"The Grangers are rich from their beef business. Everything else on their land is extra. I guess it's how Larry always wanted things, and since he had Liam and local help, it was easy enough to keep so much going. And then with Betsy's big vision..." Penny shrugged and finished off another cookie.

Molly shook her head. Why did she even care? Oh, right. The baking competition. "There'll be more contests, anyway," she said at last.

Penny looked up but not at Molly. Someone else was coming back into the kitchen. By this time, it could be kitchen staff preparing for the day. Or Molly's students.

"Hi, Dad!" Penny waved her frosting bag at Molly's

boss. Penny then whipped around to Molly. "Look!" she hissed.

Molly squinted to see there was someone else with Mr. Porter.

Penny added, "I *told* you."

Chapter 7 — Molly

Molly braced for impact, but once the principal neared the kitchen, her little helper, Penny, cheered up. "Hi, Ms. Granger! Have you tried Miss Maison's sugar cookies yet? They are. So. Good." The teen girl rolled her eyes in mock ecstasy.

The woman gave Penny a toothy grin. "Why, no, I haven't! But do you know what, Penny Porter? I'd love a sample." She bent her arm and swung it in front of her like she was gearing up for some adventure. Then she took her fist and offered it as a hand to Molly. "You must be the famous Ms. Molly Maison! I have heard *so* much about you."

If Molly wasn't seeing things, there was a suspicious twinkle in the woman's eye.

They shook and Molly feigned humility and said, "And I've heard a lot about you too." She avoided exchanging a look with Penny, which took great effort.

"You two are busy in here!" Ms. Granger added.

It occurred to Molly that maybe that's why the two had

come. "Oh! Right. Yes. We're making cookies today. I already reserved the cafeteria for this morning on through lunch. We're staying out of the lunch ladies' ways. I *promise*," she assured both of them. Maybe Betsy was on the school board.

"Oh, no no *no*, dear!" Betsy trilled sharply. "You do your cooking. You can have the kitchen all day!" *On what authority?* Molly wanted to ask. *And what about lunch?* Something smelled fishy about this interruption.

"Thank you," she said, instead.

Mr. Porter gave a short cough. "Actually, we came around because of the school board meeting last night."

"School board meeting?" *On a Sunday night?*

Betsy must have read Molly's mind. "We had an executive session. It came up because of some community concerns." She pursed her lips and waved her hands like an air traffic controller. "Not concerns about *you*, dear."

Waves of worry tossed Molly's stomach. She never should have stolen a few bites of that cookie dough. "Oh. Okay." It was hard to sound hopeful.

"Penny, you need to get to class," Mr. Porter commanded abruptly, checking his watch. Indeed, behind him, students were emerging in the distance, beyond the cafeteria, trudging across the halls like zombies.

"This *is* my class, Dad." Still, she grabbed her backpack and slinked out from the kitchen to the cafeteria tables, where Molly would begin class.

Molly cleared her throat. "Is everything okay, Mr. Porter?" She shot a steely look at Betsy. "Ms. Granger?" For being a busybody, according to Penny, it was suspect that Molly hadn't seen this lady a single time in the two months since she began teaching or the *three* months since she'd moved into her apartment in town.

Molly checked herself. It was only two months ago that Betsy had lost her brother to the heart attack.

The small woman knitted her fingers together. Her eyes, bright blue orbs behind floral framed glasses, squinted and she shook her head as if, *no*, everything was not alright.

"So I *can't* have the cafeteria today?"

Mr. Porter hitched up his pants. "Ms. Maison, the facts are, the community never wanted a culinary program. They want agriculture. We found a way to make that happen, and it's all thanks to *you*."

Molly's heart stopped. Her body went rigid, as if turning from human to robot. Her neck ratcheted tightly until she was looking at Mr. Porter. Molly narrowed her eyes like lasers on him. "*Excuse* me?"

He stammered, "The...um...the fact is, kiddo, we hired you as a long-term substitute for four elective periods. Cooking was a great start. And Penny sure loves you!" He tried to laugh. "Anyhow, a couple o' parents are gung ho about their boys taking agriculture on account of college scholarships. Did you know the Midwest boasts some of the best farming programs?" He hitched his belt as if it was a point of pride for *him*, which made no sense. "Anyhow, this isn't immediate."

Molly's mouth had gone dry, and her words shriveled up on the desert of her tongue. She managed to ratchet her head back to Betsy, who looked sheepish.

"Sweetheart," Betsy said, "You can teach through Christmas. We'll start you in the agriculture program in January. Anyway, harvest is over."

Molly managed a blink. "I don't know anything about agriculture."

Mr. Porter must have taken that as an encouraging sign because a big fat smile rippled across his lips. He reached his arm around Betsy and pulled her into him. Being as petite as she was, she nearly fell, but her wits were about her and her amusement too. She smiled and laughed like all was well. "That's where the Granger Ranch comes in."

Chapter 8 — Liam

The alarm had been going off for over a minute at the Granger Ranch.

Liam groaned beneath his covers. Every morning for the past eight weeks, he'd woken up to that sound wishing he could just roll over and smack the top of a clock to quieten it.

Roosters didn't have a snooze feature, though.

At the foot of his bed, Georgie barked once. Twice. Little yelps that were the cattle dog's way of checking on his master. After his dad's death, Liam had moved the old man's chest from his room at the back of the house to where Georgie now sat and wagged his tail. It was a large wooden thing that, if belonging to a woman, might have been a hope chest. But it was Larry's, and inside was every last important document and memento the man had ever kept. Liam only knew as much because when Larry was alive, Liam sometimes watched the man put a certificate into it or a special pipe—the one from when Larry's dad passed.

When Larry died, though, Liam didn't want to crack it open. Still, he knew it would one day be an important task, which was why he was sure to bring it into his own bedroom, cover it in a thick wool blanket, and ensure it remained safe in his possession. Georgie must have had the instinct to understand because atop that chest was where the dog found himself night after night.

Liam groaned again and rolled over, pulling a pillow onto his head and tugging it down tight over his ears.

The sound of Leroy-the-Rooster didn't stop, though. It made its way through the windows and pillow, and directly into Liam's brain, triggering what had become a nearly constant headache.

There hadn't been a single, headache-free day since his father's death. Only when Liam slept was he free from the pain.

The cooing sound came again.

"Come *on*!" He ripped the pillow from his head and pushed his fingers hard through his overdue-for-a-haircut locks. It had become a mop, according to Betsy, who offered to give him a trim. But he was on strike.

From haircuts? she'd asked.

From life, he'd answered.

Except bacon.

His stomach growled and he squinted at the non-alarm clock. Eight in the morning.

Liam turned his scowl to the window. It was too late for Leroy to be cock-a-doodle-dooing. Not by much. Now that it was on into November, the sun didn't see fit to drag herself above the plains in Prairie Creek until well after seven.

But eight?

The shrill sound came again, and that's when Liam realized it wasn't Leroy. It was his doorbell. A kitsch thing Betsy thought was hilarious on account of exactly what was happening right now. Liam was mistaking it for the sound of his rooster's morning cries.

Speaking of Betsy—if the doorbell was going off, then surely she was aware someone was there? She might live in a different cabin on the property, but Betsy wasn't quite as affected by Larry Granger's death. She'd managed to keep living. Betsy woke up in the morning. She showered. She ate a healthy breakfast and left through her front door to get the mail and make sure the goats hadn't eaten the barn, and the horses hadn't gone wild.

Somebody had to, anyway.

Liam blinked through the bleariness of a long, long sleep. Georgie yipped at him again, then cocked his head. *We've got company*, the dog reminded him.

"I know." He launched himself up and out of bed, swinging his legs over the side and stabilizing himself for a moment. At his bedside was a half-empty glass of water and a bottle of aspirin. He swallowed two without the water.

Company.

Long gone were the mourners and casserole pushers. Any company of late had been people who'd started to wonder if it wasn't Liam who fell off the face of the earth rather than Larry.

"I'm alive," Liam assured Georgie as the dog came to him for morning pets. After a good ear scrub, Liam stood, wobbly on his feet as he wandered through the house and toward the front door.

En route there, he grabbed a carton of orange juice from the fridge. Thank goodness for Betsy, or else Liam *would* have perished too. She kept him in OJ and bacon—both store bought.

He chugged for a moment as the insufferable rooster chime went off again. "Coming!" he called hoarsely, running the back of his hand across his mouth.

Liam glanced through the windows in the door to see the mottled shape of a stranger, probably.

He wondered if it was best to ignore the person altogether. Liam could go back to sleep. Wake up and air fry some bacon to get him through another grueling day of nothingness.

Then came the knocking. Incessant, ornery knocking, as if it was a little neighbor kid coming around to bug him.

"I'm coming!" Liam repeated.

He wrenched the door open, and his initial suspicions were confirmed. A stranger.

Or...*wait*.

She wasn't a stranger. Not exactly.

Chapter 9 — Molly

Liam Granger looked...*different*. Gone were the snug-fitting jeans and cuffed flannel shirt. In their place, a well-worn hoodie with a college name. Comfy-looking sweats. Molly's eyes traced down his form, but she looked away as soon as her gaze landed below his waist. Suffice it to say the sweats were a touch more revealing than sturdy jeans.

She felt herself turn red in the neck and cheeks. "I'm sorry to bother you." Molly leveled her gaze on his face, and pinned it there, which was also hard to do.

She'd obviously woken him up, but despite the overall rumpled look, Liam Granger emanated an indescribable quality. If she were less annoyed, she'd call it charm. But Molly was extremely annoyed to be there. She crossed her arms, then uncrossed them. He'd just lost his dad. He didn't deserve her scorn, even if she couldn't contain it.

"It's Molly, right?" He raked his hand through his hair.

"Yes. Molly. From the school."

"Culinary Arts."

"Not anymore."

He lifted an eyebrow.

"It's...wait. You don't know?" She peered beyond Liam into the house. The inside appeared to match the outside. All mahogany wood and forest green touches. It was very much a man's cabin. The log siding was waxen with finish, shined to within an inch of its life. Thick white chinking, too, looked to have been recently redone, or whatever it is you do with chinking.

The front porch was broad and offered a menagerie of rocking chairs—different sizes and colors. Molly imagined Liam and his dad sitting out there, clinking beer bottles, and reveling in just how much of God's green earth they owned.

What she could see inside the cabin was a mirror image of the outside, except more leather and antlers. An antler chandelier hung just above Liam's head. A cowhide throw draped over the back of a worn leather sofa. Two mismatched leather armchairs helped the sofa to frame a braided rug. A big-screen TV hung above the fireplace. Maybe Liam and his dad *did* celebrate Black Friday at one point.

Liam followed Molly's eyes. He rubbed the back of his head. "Um. Did you want to come in?"

She fell back a step, then looked over her shoulder. Where were the others? Mr. Porter was supposed to meet her here. Ms. Granger too.

"I might look dangerous," he said, "but he's the one you really have to worry about." Liam threw a thumb over his shoulder, and Molly noticed for the first time a gorgeously groomed dog. Black, white, and the color of hazelnut, sitting as still as a statue.

Molly couldn't control herself. She fell to her knees and called the pup over, clicking her tongue and patting the tops of her thighs. "Hi, there!" she cooed in a baby voice. "Look at you, you beautiful girl!"

"*Boy*," Liam interjected. "This is Georgie."

"Georgie! You sweet, sweet boy, you. Hello!" Molly ruffled the fur under his collar and let the happy dog lick her up the side of her face as she laughed and felt—for the first time all week—something akin to happy.

Georgie gave a quick, sharp *yip* and backed up, then barked again. He repeated this three more times until he was backed all the way into the cabin, and Molly was left on her knees at the threshold.

Liam began to walk off. "Do you take cream with your coffee?"

Chapter 10 — Liam

Seeing Molly Maison again was like getting a kick to the groin.

She reminded him of one thing and one thing only—the moment he got the call that would change his life forever. And the distraction that kept Liam from focusing on what counted—keeping tabs on his aunt and dad. If Liam hadn't been so content to sit at Betsy's table and steal peeks at the Culinary Arts teacher across the way, maybe he'd have gone home. Maybe he'd have found his dad in time.

Maybe everything would be different.

Even so, if there was one thing Larry Granger taught Liam, it was to respect women. As a young boy growing up, this advice was confusing. After all, Larry's own wife—Liam's *mom*—had abandoned them both just after Liam was born. Who could respect *that*?

But anytime Liam asked anything about it, Larry shut him down, insisting that despite it all, his mom was a good woman and that she *would* have been a great mother.

Pfft.

Now here was Liam, totally alone save for the only other woman or person in his life, Aunt Betsy. And she was another breed. Yes, she was a good person. And she loved Liam to pieces. He loved her back. But Betsy was a tough nut to crack, to use her own words.

Liam set about filling the coffee pot with water, then struggled to get a filter from the stack. The pads of his fingers were dry as a bone. He eyed the fridge, willing there to be some bacon still inside.

Once the coffee was set, he moved to the fridge to check.

Empty as a desert basin in June. *Dang it*.

Liam looked over at Molly next.

Her dark hair was parted down the middle and plaited on both sides. Overalls swallowed up her body, and beneath those a black-and-white flannel shirt. Over the whole ensemble she wore an oversize Carhartt jacket, complete with a tag hanging off the hem. On her feet, sneakers. She looked ridiculous.

And adorable.

And it made his stomach flip. Or maybe that was the hunger talking.

Awkwardly, he put his hands together and sort of announced, "So."

Molly was still on the floor with Georgie, petting him to his heart's content and spoiling him rotten.

"He's so beautiful, seriously."

"Thanks. They say he gets his eyes from me."

Molly didn't laugh. Instead, she stood and gave Georgie one last, rueful look. "I actually came around expecting to meet your aunt and Mr. Porter. I figured they'd told you about everything."

"Right. Some big news." Liam yawned and closed the fridge, still in denial over its emptiness. The smell of coffee grounds filled the air, sumptuous and energizing in and of itself. "Let me guess. The school wants to buy the ranch and build on it."

"I don't think so. But, maybe?" She shrugged. "Do you have pumpkin spice creamer?"

At that, Liam laughed. "I don't even have milk."

"You offered creamer." Her tone was as bitter as fresh cranberries.

"Yeah. I wasn't thinking."

"Do you *ever*?"

"Ever what?" Liam was rummaging for powdered milk in a high cabinet now.

"Ever *think*?"

He turned. She was standing, arms crossed. She seemed to do that a lot, and it was beginning to aggravate him. "You don't know me, you know," he reminded her. "You have no idea whether I'm one of the great thinkers of the world. So far as you know, they're working on carving my face into Mount Rushmore right this very minute." He threw her a sidelong gaze.

She didn't flinch. "I know why I'm here, though, and I can't imagine for one second that *you* don't."

"You think I'm lying."

"At least I'm thinking."

Liam reached up and flipped the cabinet door closed. It hit more loudly than he planned.

Molly flinched. "I'm sorry. It's just...I don't get it."

"Yeah, me neither. Otherwise, maybe I could help you understand whatever it is you don't get." He didn't mean a word of it.

Molly sighed. "I'm sorry about your dad."

It was an inch too far. "You know what? Forget the coffee. Forget the powdered milk. I think you should go."

Concern spread over her wide-open features. Maybe she was being sincere, but Molly Maison didn't have any business even *mentioning* Liam's father.

She remained in place, though. Frozen or stubborn. Probably both.

Liam held his hand toward the door. "You can head over to Betsy's cottage. It's less than a hundred yards north. You can't miss it. White paint and pumpkins all over the place. She can help you with whatever it was you needed."

"Really, Liam. I'm *sorry*." She looked down at Georgie, and he could see the temptation to bend and pet, but Liam was adamant. He whistled short and low. Georgie came over instantly and sat beside Liam. "Good to see you, Molly."

Chapter 11 — Molly

Heat rushed up Molly's spine as she walked to the front door. It curled around onto her neck like a stranglehold, and more than likely splotches of red had bloomed over her chest—Molly's hallmark sign of personal embarrassment.

Liam Granger was even worse than she thought.

She didn't say so much as a goodbye to Liam, but she did manage a discrete wave to Georgie, the only real gentleman in this cabin.

As she opened the front door and moved down the porch steps, Molly tried to remind herself that Liam was hurting. He was grief stricken. What if Molly's mother died? She'd be in full witch mode for the better part of a decade.

Even so, it made no sense that Liam would not be in the loop on Mr. Porter's grand plans for P.C.H.S. and Granger Ranch. How could he, even with Betsy's help, keep mum for a whole week? How could they let Molly show up without them and make a fool of herself?

She was beginning to wonder why she didn't take the other option, *leave Prairie Creek*. What did a long-term substitute's contract matter, anyway? Nothing, that's what. Molly could get a teaching job anywhere. Probably a Culinary Arts one too.

But then...she recalled Penny. Sweet Penny who'd started talking about going to school for baking and opening her own pastry shop one day. And Molly recalled the unruly farm boys in her class. The ones who, apparently, were set to have their college tuition covered, if only they could fulfill credits first. They were raucous, sure. They smelled like chewing tobacco half the time, yes. And they failed every single measurement and utensils test Molly had ever given, but...they had fun. They'd cooked things. Parker Porter himself had managed to make a roast chicken *without* burning it. Molly's program was flourishing in spite of everything.

She could leave and do the same thing somewhere else, yes.

Or she could stay and try to win back what she'd already begun. She had until December, at the very least. Who knew what could happen after that? Maybe the school board would come around? Maybe the families would come around? Maybe even her own students would fight for Molly and the culinary program.

Molly might not have the job she wanted in the long term, no. But right now? Well, she had *hope*. And that was more than could be said for many people.

Besides, as her mother so often reminded her, Molly's apartment rent was paid up through May, courtesy of her dad's saved up child support. And with Jean Maison on a teacher's salary herself, there wasn't enough extra cash to go around. So...it was move back home with Mom in Aberdeen, or stay through her lease.

Molly stood on a carpet of frosted grass. The week had warmed up, only just enough to burn off that early winter's snow, but the mornings were cold as ever. Too cold for Molly to shed the jacket she'd found at Goodwill. It was pricey for something secondhand, but the clerk had assured her that Carhartt was a name brand and, as a South Dakotan, Molly probably should have heard of it by now.

Oh well.

She trudged through the grass and over the frozen dirt lane that served as a drive and across toward the only other home looking structure on the property. Though the walk was short by normal standards, it felt weird to walk from one house to another on a single property.

Despite her upbringing in Aberdeen, which was another relatively small town—compared to Chicago, for example—Molly hadn't had the outdoorsy experiences of other northerners. She'd lived in the same house as her mother and father and grandmother. Then, when her parents divorced, she and her mom stayed on in the Maison house, where Molly worked fastidiously to cling to all she learned from her mimi.

Molly couldn't go half a day without thinking about the woman who'd taught her all she'd known about cooking.

Mimi adored Molly and trained her in the kitchen, braided her hair, taught her the little French Molly knew, and all of the cooking. After Molly's dad had left them, Molly and her mom had stayed on in the Maison house up in Aberdeen. Hard feelings hadn't washed over from the divorce, and Mimi had treated Jean Maison like a daughter even after. This alone had taught Molly a thing or two about loving someone even when things were complicated.

"Why, hello, Molly!" A bright voice rattled Molly from her reverie. She looked up to see Ms. Granger leaving her cottage. "You made it."

"Is Mr. Porter here yet?"

"Oh, right. He called to say he couldn't make it." Ms. Granger's face drew in. "I'm sorry. Did you get to talk to Liam?"

"Yes and no."

The woman cocked her head and frowned.

"He said he didn't know why I was here. He seemed confused. Like he isn't...*in* on the plan?"

"You didn't tell him?"

At that, Molly stopped.

Liam really *didn't* know about the plan. This changed something for her. Not the edge she felt toward him because he was a total jerk. And because even if he wasn't the one to come up with the grand idea, he was still innately involved.

"No," she answered. "Was I supposed to tell him?" Was it *Molly's* job to explain to Liam Granger everything that was going on?

But Ms. Granger waved her off. "He'll figure it out. Come on, hon, follow me. I'll give you the grand tour!"

Chapter 12 — Liam

L iam stood at the front window of his cabin and watched Molly. Georgie pawed at his leg. "She's awful," he said to the dog. "Let Betsy deal with her."

Georgie yelped.

"I know *you* like her, but I don't."

Georgie whined and jogged to the front door, pawing.

"No." Liam was going to put his foot down on this.

Georgie pawed again.

"You're going to scratch the varnish on that, then you'll really be sorry, bud," Liam's tone sharpened, but that only seemed to make Georgie yip and paw harder.

"You have *got* to be kidding me." Liam looked out the window to see Molly had met Betsy. Good. Then they could handle whatever Molly's business was.

He kept his eye on the women. Their forms were small against the browned November landscape, but he could see clear as day they both turned from Betsy's cottage and were growing larger by the moment.

"Oh no. What is she *doing*?" Liam asked Georgie.

The dog's tail wagged in excitement. He pawed the door and barked louder. "Oh, so you're in on this?"

Sure enough, Betsy was walking Molly directly back to his cabin. To Liam. And Georgie too.

"You really are going to scratch the varnish." Liam sighed and opened the door, releasing Georgie to the porch, but the dog took off down the steps and barreled over frosty ground toward the women.

Good, Liam thought. *I hope you tackle her to the ground and she never comes back*. It was a cruel thought, but those were the only kind Liam managed to conjure lately.

"Liam Lawrence Granger." Betsy's hands were on her hips and she was up on the porch before Liam could pour his first cup of coffee.

Behind her, Molly was kneeling on the ground, rubbing Georgie and spoiling him rotten. Liam scowled at the traitorous pooch.

"Now what?" He wasn't about to let his drink cool, so he sipped slowly and kept one eye over the rim, monitoring Molly.

"She came here for *you*."

"For me?" He could have spat the hot liquid out on a rough laugh, but he wasn't that awful. "Well, that's news."

"Everything is news to you because you hardly leave this cabin, much less the property." Betsy pursed her lips and looked over her shoulder, directing her next thought to Molly. "He's been a mess since Larry passed." Betsy looked back at Liam, her eyes free of sympathy but not altogether empty of compassion. "It's time, Liam."

He shifted uncomfortably in his comfortable sweats. "Time for what?"

"Time to start getting ready for the Holiday Festival."

He recoiled, shook his head, and firmly answered, "No. Not happening this year."

"Oh, yes it is. If you want this ranch to keep on, then you'll have it."

"The ranch can do just fine without selling canned jam, Bets. Sorry to tell you."

"Oh, really? Because you've sold half the livestock."

"I didn't do that. Dad's *death* did that." This was half true. Once Larry died, the buzzards came around. For every friend who dropped off a casserole, a stranger dropped off an offer to buy Liam out. By mid-October, he'd succumbed to several, saying goodbye to the better part of his beef cows, every last one of his horses save for Dina, and a few goats and pigs. All Liam had left were the bare basics. It was no question that Liam's income was now stagnant. All he had was the money from those sales and the property which he couldn't seem to leave. Oh, and Georgie and the chickens. He couldn't seem to *give* the chickens away.

"No. You did that. And if we want to keep things status quo around here, then the festival is key."

Liam shrugged. Maybe she was right. "Okay. Fine, then. If you want to carry on with the festival, that's all right by me."

"Great!" Betsy lit up. "Molly, come on in here, dear."

The porch door batted open, and Georgie and Molly entered together, her hand never leaving him.

"Molly's going to help us." Betsy's phone rang, and she answered it, wandering off to the back of the cabin and chatting away as if she didn't just bring a stranger back into Liam's house, leaving them alone together.

So *that's* why Molly had shown up. Betsy convinced her to come and help the poor fool who lost his dad and was on a downward spiral of bad financial decisions.

Humiliating.

Liam moved his gaze to his coffee, pretending to examine it. His stomach growled. "I appreciate the offer, but Betsy and I can manage."

"Actually, it wasn't my idea."

When he looked up, he realized Molly was flinching and as anxious as him, and he had the thought that she wasn't only petting Georgie because he was an attention hound, but because she needed something to do with her hands.

"Oh." Liam sipped the last of his coffee. "Did you want coffee now?"

"No. Thanks." She stood. Georgie whined. "Sorry, boy. I, um—where did your aunt go?"

Liam shrugged. "She paying you to be here or something?" Another thought occurred to him. "I don't need anyone to cook for me."

Fire lit up Molly's face. Her big brown eyes glowered at him, and her entire posture changed—her shoulders rolled back, arms folded over her chest, and right boot tapping the wood floor. "I am *not* cooking for you."

"All done!" Betsy reappeared. "I take it you two are all set, then?"

Liam and Molly remained staring at each other. A standoff.

The only answer Betsy got was another yip from Georgie.

"Look, Liam, it's not *my* choice, and it's not Molly's. She's going to work here, and so are her students. It's settled, sweetheart."

Liam wrenched his stare from Molly and her steely set jaw to look at his aunt. "Students?"

Molly replied, "Principal Porter wants me to teach agriculture next semester."

Somewhere deep down, Liam knew what this meant for the new teacher. But on the surface, he was mainly curious about the implications regarding the ranch. "What does that have to do with me?" he asked, doubling down on his self-centered apathy.

"You *really* don't know?" Molly's tone turned to sour acid.

Even Betsy gave him a look. "Your dad signed this before he passed. *Liam,* Prairie Creek High School and Granger Ranch have entered into a contract. You're going to train Miss Maison on how to run a ranch. In return, her students will help with the festival."

Liam's jaw dropped. *Train* her? The woman who hates him?

But when he looked at Molly, he saw two things. One, she was as embittered by the plan as he was.

And two, she looked terribly cute in Carhartt.

Chapter 13 — Molly

They had left Liam behind, and Betsy had given Molly a full tour of the Granger grounds. Georgie joined them too. He was quickly becoming Molly's second favorite friend in town, apart from Penny. And yes, she realized how pathetic that truly was.

By the time they wrapped up their jaunt, Molly spied Liam mucking out the stables.

Her first thought was how dang handsome he looked changed out of sweats and into Wranglers. Her second thought was how he'd looked just as hot in sweats. And her third thought wasn't fit for thinking.

Molly shook all three notions from her head and instead forced herself to focus not on Liam or the pretty pinto who neighed from the tall red barn and instead on her own goal. Get through the next two weeks without giving up, because cleaning a chicken coop was going to be way, *way* harder than kneading dough on a marble slab. Stinkier too.

But even if Molly was annoyed beyond measure with her soon-to-be assignment, she couldn't deny the excitement boiling up inside her.

When she returned to school the next day, she sat down at her desk calendar to think through what the next couple of weeks and months might look like.

Two weeks until the festival—which meant two weeks of teaching baking, acquiring ingredients and supplies, actually baking, packaging, and prep.

And about six weeks until Christmas.

Six weeks during which she'd be spending her Monday through Friday afternoons playing student, rather than teacher. Student of *Liam Granger*, for goodness' sake. And *outside,* on the frigid prairie. Ugh.

At least, she had the holidays themselves to look forward to.

Her mother would come down, and they'd go look at Christmas lights. It was then that Molly intended to spill the beans to her mom. She dreaded it. Not only would her mom be disappointed *in* Molly, even worse, she'd be disappointed *for* Molly.

After Christmas, Molly would have even more work ahead of her. She'd have to move into her new classroom on the other side of campus. She'd set it up as well as possible. She'd organize the weekly field trips to the ranch where the freezing mission would carry on. She'd find a way to complete these field trips and *not* have to interact with Liam Granger anymore. Hopefully, by then, she'd know all she'd need to know to pull off a semester of agriculture. A spring of preparing the land and planting and doing whatever else farmers or ranchers did in the veritable tundra.

After all of that, Molly would go to the school board with an ultimatum—give her back her Culinary Arts classes or kiss Prairie Creek High's new favorite teacher goodbye forever.

Of course, Molly still needed to actually *become* the students' favorite teacher.

At least she was one student's...

Sure enough, Penny Porter arrived at class early. Her arms were weighed down with an awkwardly shaped object wrapped in brown paper and tied off in a big red bow.

"What's this?" Molly stood up, tucking her pencil behind her ear.

Penny hefted it up onto Molly's desk. "An early Christmas present."

"Christmas? For *me*?"

"I found it at the Shoo Fly Shop, and I remember you talking about that cobbler we could make for the festival."

Molly didn't deserve to have a student *this* sweet. But who was she to complain? She needed all the kisser-uppers she could possibly get.

She untied the ribbon and let the thick brown paper fall open. "Oh, Penny!" Molly held up a large, heavy cast iron pan, admiring it and beaming at Penny. "This is amazing!"

"You said we'd need one."

"I could have bought it."

"I wanted to get it for you." Penny's eyes turned sad. "But I hope it doesn't become, like, a *goodbye* present."

"Goodbye? Do you *want* me to leave?"

At that, Penny burst into teenage tears. "No!" she wailed. "I'm worried you're not going to come back to Prairie Creek after this school year."

Her heart touched, Molly reached across her desk and squeezed Penny's arm. "Don't be silly. I'm not going anywhere."

"Not now, maybe."

"And maybe not next year, either."

Penny pulled back and looked up at Molly. "How come?"

"I have an idea."

At the very end of the school day, Molly packed her tote and left promptly. Normally, she stuck around to tidy up and prepare for the next day, but daylight wouldn't wait around, and she had a new after school commitment—ag training.

On her way out to the Granger Ranch, Molly made a detour onto Main Street, where she stopped for a hot cocoa, thickly topped in whipped cream. She was about to leave when she realized she couldn't very well show up to her first day with a treat for herself and nothing for her new instructor. Begrudgingly, she stalked back to the counter and asked for a second.

With both drinks secured in a sturdy paper cupholder, she was off in her little white car, rolling back down Main and north toward the ranch.

She arrived five minutes past four. The sun was bleeding down to the horizon.

No sign of Liam.

With the quickly cooling drinks, one in each hand, she took off around the side of the main cabin, peering through the slicing rays of sinking sun. The barn appeared empty from where she stood by a lone haystack. So did the pigsty—was that what they were *actually* called? The chicken coop was aflutter with testy birds. Out in the distance, goats grazed lazily. Beyond them, cows lowed. It was every bit the idyllic prairie ranch scene. If only Molly could enjoy it as that instead of as a worker. Not that she couldn't work, but this was not her idea of a fulfilling career.

A sound came from behind. Molly swiveled in time to brace for impact.

"Georgie, no!" she shrieked just in time for the excitable dog to barrel into her. Without the use of her hands, she couldn't self-stabilize, but in an effort to keep her drinks from spilling, she ended up thrusting backward. Georgie didn't stop his offensive, and soon enough, the back of Molly's thighs hit the haystack and back she went, sailing, heels over head with Georgie, unrelentingly affectionate, licking her face on the far side of the hay.

A low, loud whistle came from somewhere in the distance. Molly wondered if it was the voice of God himself, calling her to heaven. But if she were dead, she probably would have dropped the hot cocoas. Yes, they were spilled— warm brown liquid and splotchy white cream dripped up into her Carhartt jacket, and her chest and stomach were soaked. But still, she had the cups and probably at least half of the drinks remained.

Georgie pushed off of Molly and dashed away. Molly gave herself another moment to take stock of the fall. Her back was jolted but fine. Her head didn't hurt. All that bothered her was the fact that she was wet with hot chocolate and the sun was going down on the prairie. She'd freeze out here. She was sure of it.

"Are you okay?"

"Georgie?" Molly murmured, looking into that setting sun and making sense of the figure barreling back at her. Maybe she *did* have a concussion.

Chapter 14 — Liam

"Are you okay?" Liam's jog turned to an all-out run when Molly couldn't lift her head to see him or raise her voice to answer him. Georgie ran beside Liam, obedient now that he realized he'd hurt someone. And not just *someone* but the girl Georgie was so in love with. "Georgie, *stay*," Liam commanded, slowing as he arrived at the haystack. He'd been in the middle of moving hay to the back hangar when he heard Molly's car approach.

He'd nearly forgotten she was coming.

Okay, that wasn't true. He'd lost track of time, yes, but he *knew* she was coming. When he realized she had arrived, Liam scrambled to drive the baler to the back of the cabin, parked it, and dashed inside to throw on a fresh shirt and gargle some mouthwash. It wouldn't do to teach someone if he wasn't entirely presentable.

"Molly, are you okay?" He knelt at her side, hesitant to touch her but worried that she was badly hurt. Stupid hay.

Stupid Georgie. As soon as Liam thought that, he took it back. Georgie wasn't stupid. Just...dumb. *Ack*. Whatever. "Are you okay?" Liam asked again, settling on putting one hand on Molly's shoulder.

She was staring at him, her brown eyes full of something. Hate? He sure hoped not. Would she sue him? "I'm really sorry about this bale. I wasn't thinking. I should have —" Should have been a normal person and *not* rushed inside to change his shirt and gargle Scope. After all, who cared if he smelled like a ranch?

"I think I'm okay." Molly moved to sit up, and it was then that Liam's eyes traced down her form. She held two to-go coffee cups. The lids were missing. He looked around to search for them to see that whatever fancy coffee drink had been inside was half-sloshed all over Molly's Carhartt jacket and beneath it, on her white blouse.

Liam quickly averted his gaze. "Here, let's get you up. Make sure you're not hurt." He took the two cups and set them on top of the hay then reached for her hands.

"I'm fine," she managed weakly.

"You don't sound fine." He didn't want to look like he was checking her out, but Liam really did worry Molly hit her head when she fell. She seemed...off.

Once she was back on her feet, she held her arms out from her body awkwardly. "I'm...sort of wet."

That's when he saw that her jacket wasn't only stained with liquid but somehow it had torn too. Her entire right sleeve had pulled from the seam at the shoulder and slipped down her arm like a saggy tube sock.

Liam reached for it, half curious about how a well-made jacket could tear so easily.

Molly took her hand and pushed the sleeve back up in place, warding his gesture off. "It was like this when I got it. I guess it had been in bad shape. The sleeve was about to come off. I don't really know how to sew. I did my best." She studied the seam proudly. "I guess my best wasn't good enough."

"Georgie." Liam clicked his tongue and shook his head in disappointment. "Look at what you've done."

Liam then cleared his throat, scratched the back of his head, and looked around as if an answer might crop up.

"Maybe I should go home." She held her sleeve in place, awkwardly.

Liam pointed out, "That'll be another twenty or thirty minutes before you can get started then. You'll throw the afternoon away."

Georgie let out a yip. "You hush," Liam warned the dog. "You've done enough for today."

"Oh. Well, can I start tomorrow?"

Liam didn't think that was a good idea, based on what Phil Porter said about Molly logging hours. Besides, it was —well, what *was* it? He lifted up one of the cups and took a whiff. "This doesn't smell like coffee."

"Well, it *was* hot chocolate."

Of course. Liam snapped his fingers. "Let me guess. The Brewster on Main?"

"Is there another beverage shop in town?"

"Not that I know of." Georgie barked again. He refused to be quieted. The dog barked a third time and angled his body toward the cabin. "What? You got your breakfast and lunch. Supper's later." Liam looked back at Molly. "Do you have spare clothes in your car, or—?"

She shook her head. "I have the sweater I wore to school, but I'd rather not work in that." A quick shake of her head. "I don't want to sound fussy. I already hate that I've spoiled this afternoon."

"I have an idea," Liam said.

Chapter 15 — Molly

"This should work." Liam passed over a small stack of neatly folded garments.

Molly said, "Thanks. And...where's the bathroom?"

"Oh, right." He ran his hand up the back of his head, buffing his blond hair before indicating a short hallway past the living room. "First door on the left. Can't miss it."

Molly ducked into the bathroom where she locked the door and pressed her back against it. She covered her face with the loaner clothes, a delayed humiliation consuming her just then. They smelled like soap. Not laundry detergent, but *soap*. Her mind flicked back to the back-to-school night and those crude, fragrant bars of soap Betsy Granger had been selling. In all likelihood, this family didn't stop at making hand soap. They probably made everything from the fruits of their land. What was *that* like? Well, Molly realized she knew what it smelled like, and she was about to know what it felt like. How much hard work it took to churn out enough goat milk for a single load of wash. How much hard work had gone into cleaning what she was about to put on.

Put *on*. A groan rumbled up from her throat, and so Molly kept the clothes there for another moment before laying them on the sink and studying herself in the mirror. She needed to get this over with, and quick. She pulled off the Carhartt jacket and its detached sleeve, tucking the extra material into a pocket for later mending.

Beneath the jacket, her white cotton shirt clung to her skin. She peeled it off and pulled a towel from a tall shelf full of them. Using the fluffy linen to pat her body dry, she considered her jeans. Only the top of them had sustained any spill. Maybe they'd dry quickly, and she could avoid the humiliation of wearing a stranger's pants—ones that were certain to be too big and too long.

Then Molly remembered the chilly breeze and dwindling daylight. She'd freeze.

Like with her shirt, she peeled off her jeans, folding them and adding them to her pile of clothes on the edge of the pedestal sink. It was then Molly saw that the cabin's charm didn't end with the knotty pine wood walls or the tongue and groove ceilings. Everything about the little homestead screamed, well, *homestead*.

Thick planks of wood spread throughout the cabin ran in the bathroom, too, straight beneath an ancient looking claw-foot bathtub with a forest green curtain that encircled it. On the nearer side of the tub stretched a braided rug— one of many that populated the wood floors of the house. None of Liam's home décor was modern or trendy, but it did have a certain something to it. Clean. Homey and cozy and woodsy. Masculine, yes, but in a way that fit.

She pulled on a clean white t-shirt of Liam's. It hung loosely, comfortably. After that came the thick, flannel lined corduroy jacket. It sheathed her like a suit of armor and rolling the sleeves up even once proved challenging. But once it was on, she was able to move around and she trusted she'd be warm.

Next came the jeans. Worn looking Levi's, the hems of which were threadbare. Once on, they draped onto her feet. She cuffed the bottoms even as the waist kept sliding down below her hips. With the jeans cuffed and one hand holding them up, she slipped her feet back into her work boots and emerged from the bathroom.

"Some help I'm gonna be," she declared, her body swallowed up in layers of men's clothing and her skin on fire with nerves.

Liam was pouring steaming liquid into two camo colored thermoses. He lifted an eyebrow.

Molly raised the bottom of the jacket to show him she was holding onto his jeans for dear life.

"Ah." He snapped his fingers. "Come with me."

Chapter 16 — Liam

L iam knew better than to invite a perfect stranger —and a pretty one, at that—into his bedroom like this. But that's where he had a length of rope.

Molly seemed to share his sentiment and remained at the door, inspecting the room with a critical eye.

"Yeah. I um—it's not much to look at, I guess." He grabbed the rope that hung near his closet. It was once part of a longer section he'd made a lasso out of. But that was back when he was a kid who found fun in rodeo games. Over the years, the rope had made its way into this project, even once playing leash for the hound dog, Georgie, when they needed to go to a vet in another town.

Molly took the rope. "Thanks." Before she turned to walk back down the hall, she added, "And, actually, I really like it."

"My bedroom?" As soon as the words were out of his mouth, Liam felt his cheeks light up in red. "It's just a room." Again, he cringed. "Anyway."

"Right, yeah. So, what are we doing first?"

* * *

Despite the weirdness of Molly wearing Liam's clothes, and the weirdness of her clothes still in his bathroom, and the weirdness of her being there at all, things were going smoothly.

He didn't have a lesson plan for the day, but with Betsy's help, he'd come up with a general schedule of what they needed to accomplish every day up until the Friday after next.

And it was a lot. Plus, the students wouldn't join Molly until the following week. Apparently, Phil wanted Molly to get the hang of things on her own so she didn't look entirely incompetent as their teacher. Liam figured this was good reasoning, but even so...the whole thing reeked of small town commotion.

"We've scaled back substantially, as you probably know. The chickens are going to be a big part of the festival." Liam was giving Molly a real tour, not the quickie that Betsy had tried to do. They'd stopped at the coop, where Leroy was squabbling at one of the hens.

"Oh, okay. Are you selling eggs?"

"Eggs, yes. We also butcher and prep one or two and roast them."

Molly's jaw physically dropped. He could see two even rows of straight white teeth. Whoever Molly was, she was no ranch girl. At least, not like any he'd seen.

"What?" he asked.

She struggled to work her mouth in order to reply. After a second, she managed, "Butcher one of them?" She bent down and stuck her fingers through the chicken wire. One of the hens pecked her way over.

"Oh, no. No, no, *no*." Liam reached down and grabbed Molly's wrist, pulling her free of the cage and back away from it.

She didn't fight him but asked, "Do they bite?"

He laughed. "No. I just don't want you to bond with them like you did with *him*." Liam hooked his thumb toward Georgie, who hadn't left Molly's side. Traitor.

"Do people actually buy the roasts?"

"Of course."

"Do they have names?"

"Well, yeah."

"How can you stand to kill pets?"

Liam cocked his head at her. "They aren't pets."

Molly looked back longingly at the chickens.

A thought came upon Liam. "You're a cook."

"Yeah."

"You know where your food comes from."

"The butcher, yes." She sighed. "I've never personally known any animal I've ever eaten."

"It's not a cruel thing, you know."

"How can you say that? Would you kill Georgie and eat him?"

"No, but that's a cultural preference. Georgie is my dog. My pet. The chickens are my livestock. Just like the pigs. The goats. The cows."

"What about her?" Molly jutted her chin toward the stable.

"Oh, Fannie. She's livestock too."

"You don't butcher and eat horses."

Liam frowned. "Are you just arguing to argue or is there a point you're coming to?"

"I'm not a vegan or anything. It's so *real*, I guess. So in your face."

"That's the humane thing. These chickens aren't brought up in tiny cages, crammed together, living in their own waste. They aren't starved or stuffed, deprived of water or bloated with it. They live long, good lives. And when it's time for one to go, we do it the right way."

Molly seemed to consider this. After a long beat, she seemed to accept her fate. "All right."

"All right?"

She nodded firmly and folded her arms over her chest. Her body beneath the heavy coat seemed a little more fragile than when it had been enveloped in her thrift store Carhartt. Maybe because the corduroy had belonged to his dad.

Chapter 17 — Molly

Night was falling over Granger Ranch, and Molly was tired. A full day of teaching took a toll in and of itself, but now they were hauling crates of mason jars from the hangar to a tractor to move into the cabin. "We do all the canning in the kitchen. Betsy helps."

"What do we can?" Molly asked Liam once the final crate was loaded and she hauled herself up into the shotgun seat.

"I'll drive you out there first, then we'll unload."

She remained quiet. In another world, Molly would be anxious to get home, take a hot bath, and snuggle into her terrycloth robe with her cat, Luna, cuddled at her feet. But despite her exhaustion and the temptation of a relaxing night ahead, she was enjoying herself with Liam on the ranch.

He drove them past the pasture where the goats grazed and took a sharp left. "The garden's this way."

Darkness enshrouded the prairie as they made another left turn behind the barn where a secret world opened. The headlights on the tractor glowed over a good quarter acre of gardens and beyond that, another acre of what looked like corn stalks or some other crop with height.

"We've harvested most everything. All that's left now are some late bloomers." Liam pointed to a row of pumpkins. "It happens."

They hopped off the tractor, and Molly let out an icy breath. After this, she really would need a hot bath. Maybe even her winter pajamas. Being outside in the late fall cold sent a chill so deep in her bones that she wondered why she hadn't applied for a position out in California or Arizona. Then she followed behind Liam and didn't feel quite as cold.

He squatted at the first gourd, a heavy looking orange thing, then pulled a multitool from his back pocket and sawed the stem before hefting it up.

Intuitively, Molly took the pumpkin, loaded it into the tractor trailer and came back, collecting seven more from Liam before they called it a night and headed to the cabin where they unloaded the mason jars. The pumpkins Liam would handle later. "You're probably exhausted."

Molly was physically, mentally, and emotionally spent.

"Yeah, it must be late."

They stood at the broad kitchen island which held one pack of mason jars. Liam had mentioned tomorrow they would can pumpkins and the rest of the store he hadn't gotten to yet. It was an awful lot of mason jars, and Molly was anxious to see what more they'd be doing.

He pushed off the butcher block countertop and swiveled to the fridge. "I was planning to heat up some supper." Liam pulled his head from the fridge and looked at her. "You want to, um, stay?"

Molly's stomach lurched at the thought, her insides hollow with hunger and roiling with something else. Hope? "Oh. Um..." she looked around for a clock, quickly realizing there was no microwave, and the stove wasn't electric. It was a woodstove with a cooktop—no digital anything.

Liam turned his arm her way. "It's just past seven."

Seven o'clock at night. Molly was usually in bed by now, drifting off to the cooking channel or a recipe book she'd found in some thrift shop. Her stomach growled.

Liam laughed. "I'd say that's a yes."

Chapter 18 — Liam

I t was funny how grief worked. For two months, Liam had dwelled in a shadow. No matter how much he'd wanted to find a patch of sunlight, the weight of despair blocked him. Even now, he still woke in the mornings expecting to see his dad out in the pasture—rain or shine, Larry Granger never stopped. Until he died.

The change was abrupt enough that Liam couldn't seem to accept his dad was gone.

Then Molly showed up, and at first, the sadness turned darker still. Heavier. More impossible to cross.

Until today.

Maybe it was Georgie and his senselessness or maybe it was seeing Molly fall. Maybe it was her very presence— persistent yet reluctant. But as soon as Liam saw her flip over the hay bale, it was as if a switch was flipped.

That patch of sunshine Liam had been wearily chasing found *him* instead.

Instead of expecting his dad to swoop in and save the day, scooping Molly up and brushing her off—Liam knew that it was his turn to be the hero. And though it was no heroic feat to help a woman onto her feet and offer her a fresh set of clothing, for *Liam*, there was courage in the act. There was bravery. There was the snapping of the rubber band that had been squeezing his heart.

There was freedom. Liam had even been able to sort through a towering pile of cleaned laundry—one of the few chores he'd managed—and found a pair of his jeans and one of his t-shirts. The true act of courage, however, was knowing that Molly needed a jacket and that his own would be so big she wouldn't be able to move. Larry Granger, though a broad man himself, was three inches shorter than his son and twenty pounds lighter. His coats would fit better. And he had a great corduroy one with Molly's name on it. Liam had even managed to fish it out of his dad's closet and hand it over without spilling one single tear.

Inside, his pain throbbed, but wasn't there something to be said about performing, at least? What was the old adage? Fake it until you make it.

Liam didn't see how he could fake much of anything, but what he could do was push through. He had his health. He had his aunt. And now, apparently, he had a dedicated ranch hand, if that's what you could call Molly. He hardly could.

Then came the afternoon of touring the grounds, loading the cases, organizing equipment. The distraction of the work helped, yes. But without the pretense of Molly's required attendance, Liam might never have found the spirit to get out there and *do* the work.

Before today, though, Liam had done one thing of his

own volition. He'd gone down to the Shoo Fly Shop and bought a loaf of bread and a fresh jar of peanut butter.

Presently, as Molly watched him futz around in the fridge, he found what he was looking for, a jar of jelly.

With it settled that she'd stay for supper, anxiety crept back up along Liam's spine. He'd never hosted a woman for dinner before. And if he knew he was going to, he'd have prepared a tri-tip roast or at least cooked up a bird. *And* if Liam knew he was going to be hosting a *cook*, then...

He couldn't control any of that now. He asked, "Do you mind terribly if we have PB&Js?"

To his surprise, Molly cracked a smile. "I'll help."

Liam watched in awe as Molly took over. First, she shed the corduroy coat, hanging it on the peg by the front door. The act was something Larry Granger would have done. Suddenly it was almost like Dad was still around, at least in spirit. The thought of that allowed Liam to relax and lean into the counter, watching this striking stranger while she conquered his kitchen as though she were right at home.

A pile of supplies sat between two cartons of mason jars. The tub of peanut butter, the jar of jelly, and the loaf of sourdough he'd bought.

"Do you have any butter?"

Liam grinned. "That's one thing I'm never short on." He returned to the fridge and withdrew a glass bowl. "Here you go."

"Oh my," Molly said, her eyes dazzling, "Is this freshly churned?"

"I think Betsy made it a week ago."

"By herself?"

Liam laughed. "We do lots of stuff by ourselves here."

"You realize you have more here than a working ranch, don't you?" She took the butter and dipped her pinky in it before tasting it. Her eyes rolled dramatically to the back of her head. "Oh *my*. This is divine." She set the butter down and pointed toward the stove. "Can you light that for me? We'll need a pan too."

Liam checked the firebox to ensure there was good kindling, then drew one of the long matches across the tinder box and lit the logs. Flames caught on instantly, and he drew the door shut.

Above the stove hung a menagerie of stainless steel pots and a single, oversize cast iron skillet which he pulled down. "What do you mean more than a working ranch?" Despite a long and physically demanding day, Liam felt his energy returning. Perhaps it was the anticipation of eating a hearty meal—or as hearty as a PB&J could be. Or perhaps there was something else stirring. Something about Molly.

She worked as she answered him, gripping a bread knife with ease and sawing into the fresh loaf, coming away with four thick slices. "You could live here, entirely secluded from the world." She traded the bread knife for a butter knife, which she found quickly in the center drawer. She dipped it into the peanut butter, spreading generous dollops onto all four pieces before pulling out a fresh butter knife and doing the same with the jelly.

"I already do."

Molly ran her index finger along the blade of the knife, sliding the glob of jelly off and popping it in her mouth.

She looked at him. "I mean, you would never have to leave here if you didn't want to."

"I don't." He half-grinned.

"You're a hermit?"

"I'm self-sufficient."

"You have a coffee maker." She pointed at the far wall of the kitchen. "So you have electricity."

"We're on the grid."

"Could you be *off* the grid?"

"If we wanted to, sure. We've got the generator. And people brewed hot drinks before electricity was invented."

"So you *do* know how to boil water?" She smirked at him.

Liam scowled back playfully. "You just pointed out that I can do it all here."

"I never said that. I said that you *have* it all here. There's a difference." With this quip, Molly picked up the peanut butter knife and did the same with it as she'd done with the jelly. Liam felt indecent watching as she again slipped the blade between her lips and pulled the cream off with her lips. Not indecent enough to look away, though.

He folded his arms over his chest and held her gaze. Ms. Molly Maison wasn't going to win this fight. No ma'am. "Is that a challenge?"

She shrugged, slid the two sandwiches onto the pan on the stove, then turned back to him. "It's an observation."

"I've made one of those myself recently."

"An observation? I'm impressed." Her face moved from defiant to impish, and he could either tell her to leave or grab her and kiss her. Plainly put, Liam was confused as all get out.

He sucked in a breath. "You *should* be. I'm…"

"Impressive? I wouldn't say that."

"Do you want to hear my observation or not?"

"I would *love* to." Her full lips turned up into a wicked smile, and her eyes danced. Was she daring him?

He hesitated a moment before saying it. Everything about their relationship demanded that he *not* cross this line. Everything in Liam's life required that he keep to himself. Grieve. Remain alone until he figured out what the future held. Even so, his mouth worked itself into the words that had no place between a teacher and his apprentice, even if they were the same age, standing in the same kitchen, about to share the same meal. "You are beautiful."

Chapter 19 — Molly

I t was all fun and games until Liam had to compliment her.

And this wasn't your average compliment.

Molly felt her cheeks and neck flash in a deep blush. She turned quickly away from him and picked up the spatula to flip the sandwiches.

"I'm sorry," he murmured behind her.

She took a breath, stilled herself for a moment, set the spatula down, and turned back to face him.

"No." Heat pulsed beneath her skin. "I—um..." She knit her eyebrows together. The proper response would be to thank Liam for his flattery; however, this was beyond flattery. Flattery was when someone made you feel good about yourself to get something. Liam had nothing to get from Molly.

Did he?

"What I mean is..." She swallowed, and her pulse raced. Short quick breaths confused her thinking. Still, Molly couldn't say how she felt. Where would it go? What would happen next? "What I mean to say is, um..."

Liam pointed past her. "Is that done?"

She turned to see smoke pouring out the backside of the pan. "Oh *crap*." She scooped out the sandwiches, sliding them onto a plate. Luckily, it was an errant drop of jelly that was burning, and not their dinner.

Of course, the jelly wasn't the only thing burning, though.

Smoke might also be trailing off of her cheeks as she tried in vain to redirect their conversation back to supper and the sandwiches and the ranch and *anything* other than what Liam thought of her...or what *she* thought of him.

He had to have picked up on her nervousness because he set about pouring two mason jar glasses of milk from a ceramic pitcher.

They made an awkward setting, standing at the empty end of the kitchen island, Molly with her plated sandwich and Liam with his.

"Cheers." He pushed her glass across the kitchen island and held up his own.

"Cheers." She picked up hers and clinked. Keeping her gaze anywhere except on Liam, Molly sipped the cool drink. Immediately, she noticed how much richer and creamier it was than her own 2% at home. An earthy aftertaste drove home exactly what she ought to have predicted. "Is this...*fresh* milk?"

Liam smiled. "Yep. Fresh from this weekend. I told you —I really *can* do it all." And then with a delicious grin, he winked at her.

Chapter 20 — Liam

The next day, Liam woke up without the help of Leroy, Georgie, or even a banging on the door.

After coffee and bacon, he made his way to the hall bathroom, where he kept his razor, and that's when he saw it—a neat pile of Molly's clothes from the night before.

It felt like a scandal. Like a secret, seeing her jeans and shirt and jacket there. He opted to move the whole set into the living room, where it could rest in plain sight on the armchair. That way, Liam would remember to return it all to Molly as soon as she came back.

He showered, shaved, pulled on a flannel shirt and jeans and set out not to the field, but to Shoo Fly.

Georgie accompanied him, riding shotgun in the green truck.

That afternoon, Molly would return, but not alone. Today marked the first day that her students would begin to join her as they embarked on their shared mission of preparing for the festival.

As such, Liam figured he needed a few things that weren't readily available at the ranch. Namely, more food— snacks, especially. Also, hot chocolate fixings. Finally, the accoutrements for setting up the barn.

Shoo Fly had all the basics, including cocoa powder, marshmallows, and some fresh fruit to be sliced and passed around during a work break.

He loaded up the truck, gave Georgie a talking to about slobbering over the seat, then headed home.

When he arrived back, Betsy was out front, walking Dina.

"Hey there, cowgirl!" Liam called to his aunt. "Where are you two headed?"

"Just a walk around the ranch. Getting ready for our guests by way of inspecting."

Liam snorted. "Guests?"

"Well, what else would you call Ms. Maison?"

"*You* told me to call her a trainee. An intern. A ranch hand." Liam narrowed his gaze, wondering not for the first time what his aunt had to do with all of this. "Anyway, Molly Maison has no choice but to show up and help. The school ripped her program away. So here we are." He didn't mean to sound quite as angry on Molly's behalf, but the more he'd gotten to know her, the more he felt bad she'd been thrown into this situation.

At his reply, Betsy bristled. "Even helpers are guests, young man. Besides, it's our job to host them as much as it is their job to help us. I look at it differently, I suppose." Betsy turned her nose up and Fannie fell in step, turning her muzzle to the sky as they both completed a quarter turn back toward the pasture.

"I guess you do," Liam muttered as he watched the pair of them saunter away. Speaking of the animals, Liam was reminded of what all he had to accomplish before Molly and her kids arrived. One of the most critical items being to drive the cattle into the northeast field. That was the sort of task that Georgie could practically do alone, and it was something he didn't plan to train anyone on.

The priority would be mucking out the hangar, cleaning, bringing in tables. After that, he'd walk Molly through tending the livestock. They were past harvest now; otherwise, she'd help him with the reaping. But some crops—especially in the veggie garden—could do with late fall planting. Then there were the machines and the fields. Lots of big picture things to sort through.

He wondered exactly what the future of the agriculture program looked like at the high school, but more than that, Liam wondered why it had come about. Who'd been the driving force? He'd heard it was the school board who'd asked for the change. Betsy was on the school board. Surely she wouldn't want to rip a culinary program out from under the heels of a new teacher? Or would she?

Liam never could pin down his aunt's reasoning. She was like a pesky bumblebee, dipping herself into one flower after another and flitting away heavily.

As he and Georgie finished the drive and Liam returned to the cabin to prep the canning, Betsy came knocking.

"Liam." She entered without waiting for him to answer the door. A maddening habit that Liam's dad hadn't minded, but it drove Liam nuts. "I have something to tell you."

He froze at the sink where he was rinsing out canning jars.

Betsy neared him with great trepidation, so much so that Georgie backed away from her. "Liam, I haven't been totally honest with you."

Liam blinked, turned off the faucet. Dried his hands. He studied her. "Okay."

"This whole agriculture program..."

"Mm-hmm," he replied slowly.

Betsy knitted her fingers together. "Well, you see, it wasn't just *anybody's* idea."

A million thoughts swirled through Liam's head. His well-meaning aunt, his feisty new apprentice, the future of P.C.H.S. and what it would mean for students. Did Liam really care? Well...it didn't matter to him whether today's teenagers had to take cooking or farming class. But if they didn't have to learn about agriculture, he knew exactly where that put him.

Back at square one. At least, with regards to his movement forward—away from his dad's death and toward something akin to...hope?

Betsy was still working her little fingers into each other, worrying her mouth in a tight line.

"Go on, Aunt Betsy. What is it?"

"It was *my* idea. Restarting agriculture. It was just something I sputtered out, and then *boom*, it took off like a flame to a field of dry grass. I didn't think I was doing harm —I didn't think through it, you see."

"You didn't think that you'd be..."

"Ruining Molly Maison's career."

Liam stayed quietly thoughtful for a moment. If Betsy

had felt she'd made a mistake, the right thing was to come clean and see about fixing it. But if Betsy were successful in fixing it—in returning the culinary program to what it was and allowing the ag program to die once and for all—then there was no reason for Molly to come around anymore.

He said at last, "What are you going to do?"

Betsy winced. "I don't know. I mean, we *do* need help with the festival…" she trailed off.

Disappointment swirled in Liam, but then a question emerged. "If you didn't want Molly to lose the culinary program, then why did you suggest it to begin with?"

Betsy sighed. "It was selfish."

By way of his own admonishment, Georgie sneezed.

Liam gave his aunt a hard look. "Selfish? As in you want the school's help?"

"That, yes…" Betsy began.

"…And?" Liam prodded.

"And I wanted you two to meet."

Liam frowned. "You wanted to set us up?"

She gave a guilty nod.

"And so you—" Liam shook his head. There were no words. This was typical Betsy, to set off an avalanche and feel bad only after it had demolished an entire village.

Liam was stuck—he could try and set things right, maybe even address the board—or he could go along with the sham and get more quality time with Molly.

The wheels in his head turned. Maybe there was a way to have his cake and eat it too. The only downside to that was if Molly happened to find out what Liam now knew.

Chapter 21—Molly

At school, Molly couldn't focus. She kept replaying the night before over and over in her mind. Liam's charm. The quiet supper. The cool, creamy milk.

The whole experience proved so enchanting that she was beginning to wonder if she might not love teaching agriculture.

Then fifth period struck. Her most difficult class—the rowdy group of boys who'd rather be plowing fields than icing a cake.

Seeing them reminded Molly, too, that she'd left her clothes at Liam's cabin. Part of her secretly liked that she'd left them—not that she'd done it on purpose, no, no. But that a piece of her was there, like a girlfriend might leave her toothbrush at her boyfriend's. A fantasy took shape in her head, and though she'd remember to retrieve her things, she didn't worry too much that they were there.

Molly forced herself to turn her mind to fifth period.

Today, they were doing something even harder than

icing a cake, though. They were learning about pie making. If there was one skill in Culinary Arts with which students struggled the most, it was pies, for some reason. Perhaps because pie making took great patience and skill—unlike with other disciplines. Sure, you could whip up a batch of cookies that didn't taste half bad—a cookie was a cookie, after all. But if you messed up a pie? There was no saving it.

Even so, the joy Molly got from watching Parker Porter pull his lattice trimmed pecan pie from the oven to find it had cooked up perfectly...Molly simply couldn't imagine she'd get as much satisfaction from anything else. Least of all watching someone like Penny milk a cow, for example.

Still, she'd accepted that she'd signed an ambiguous contract. That she'd gotten to teach Culinary Arts at all was a miracle, and especially in a great town like Prairie Creek. Besides, she wasn't done fighting for her program yet. She'd spend this semester following her directives— and getting to know Liam Granger. After that, she'd pursue her original claim. She'd find a way to make sure that once next school year's contracts came around, Principal Porter himself would be begging Molly to stay on and teach her passion. They'd find someone else for agriculture.

During the last few minutes of fifth period, Molly received a terse email from Principal Porter, though. Instead of her spending time ahead of her students at the ranch, they'd learn along side her. This would provide for a head start on resuming the ag program. But rather than being disappointed, Molly was a bit relieved. Having students with her would perhaps make things a bit less awkward. She didn't know a thing about ag, but she knew how to handle teenagers, and this would give her at least a tad bit of edge on things.

After reminding every class that today was field hours day at the ranch, she called the office to find out who had filled out a permission slip signed by their parent to accompany her to the ranch. They were taking one of the district's minibuses from the school to the Granger Ranch and back. Whoever signed up would get extra credit in science class, and Molly was quickly learning just how much the agriculture program—or *future* agriculture program—was valued.

The school secretary said that three students were signed up: Parker Porter, Dwayne Smith—Parker's best friend—and Penny Porter. Naturally.

Molly thanked her, slipped into her workroom closet and quick changed out of her teaching smock and into a set of warm work clothes.

They arrived at the ranch after a bumpy journey down the dirt roads that dumped out at Liam's cabin. Molly desperately wished she'd packed a compact to double-check her teeth for food and her hair for frizz. But it was too late now, and soon enough she and her trio of volunteers were piling out.

The day had turned from cold to colder, and Molly regretted not having packed gloves too.

Liam and Betsy greeted them at the porch with a serving tray of to-go cups.

"Liam mentioned you like hot cocoa," Betsy said to

Molly in particular. "It's my favorite too." Then, she winked at Molly.

Liam must have seen or read into the overture because he clapped his hands together, then gave longwinded instructions about how they were going to start with the hangar out back. After all, everything they were going to learn would also benefit both parties—the ranch would get help setting up the festival, and the culinary students would lay claim to the best booth in the hangar. Not to mention the training hours for Molly and service hours for the kids.

Instantly, Parker and Dwayne adhered themselves to Liam, showing a sharp focus and concern that Molly hadn't seen in them in the past three months she'd known either boy.

Meanwhile Penny hung back with Molly, and Betsy sidled up too. "Liam and I are *so* happy to have you here, *really*," Betsy said, her words full of a desperate emotion that suggested some degree of sympathy for Molly. Sympathy or...gratitude? Maybe the ranch really did need more help. Betsy added, "If there is anything I, personally, can do to help you feel at home, please don't hesitate." Betsy squeezed Molly's arm.

Penny said, "Ms. Granger, do you have any idea *why* the school is making Ms. Maison *do* this?"

Molly choked on her hot cocoa, sputtering through a small sip as Betsy fumbled to reply. "It's all my fault, really it is—it's just, well, you know small town politics and this, that, and the other—no one is ever happy with the way things are! Or with change for that matter!"

Molly didn't understand how any of that was Betsy Granger's fault. So far as she knew, Betsy Granger hadn't had a thing to do with the agreement. Then again, it had been Betsy who'd taken Molly under her wing that first day.

"It's really okay," Molly assured her and Penny both. "I don't mind learning about where my food comes from. It's an important part of a culinary program. I think that when it's all said and done, I'll come out a better teacher. One way or the other."

Betsy seemed satisfied by this assurance and fell back a step, busying herself with a wayward goat who'd wandered up to them.

Penny, who was generally unaware they'd even left the school, continued babbling away about a recipe for borscht her Nana Linski used to make and how it'd be the perfect addition to their festival fare.

Molly was about to give up on reminding Penny that they were hosting a bake-off—no soup—when Liam fell back a step. "I love a good borscht," he announced. "Maybe we could make that for the community dinner, Penny?"

"Community dinner?" Molly frowned up at him. "Sorry?"

"After the festival, it's customary that each business donates whatever goods they have left for a raffle for our community dinner. We put it on for anyone who needs a place at the table for the holidays. I think of it as part goodwill and part selfish. We get to help people and in return, we get a house full of warm bodies and grateful hearts." He was quiet a moment. Then, "It used to be that my dad and I roasted a turkey. Betsy would do the mashed potatoes, dressing, and some greens."

Molly nodded. She wondered how Liam was going to

get through the holidays without his dad. She couldn't imagine his pain. Her heart ached for him.

As they neared the hangar, Liam cast a sidelong look at Molly. He cleared his throat. "Shoo Fly Shop usually donates baked goods, so you don't have to worry too much about donating whatever your kids make."

"Shoo Fly Shop? Do they have a booth with baked goods?"

"Ordinarily, yes." The boys had already disappeared into the hangar. Liam turned to face Molly. "I told the owner this morning that we had another baked goods booth that the school was hosting."

Molly chewed on her lower lip. "I don't want to step on any toes. I can't afford to make anyone mad right now."

He shook his head, adamant. "You're not making anyone mad. Trust me." His eyes glimmered with an unspoken promise. Or was it something else? Was Molly seeing in Liam what she *wanted* to see? Or was there a lie behind those cornflower blue eyes? Was he setting her up to fail? Would she arrive at the festival with her students and their pies only to meet with the frowning faces of the good townsfolk of Prairie Creek?

Instead of pressing him for an explanation, she asked, "Who else has a booth at the event?"

Liam laced his fingers and stretched his arms out in front of him. "Come on in, and I'll show you the event plan."

Inside the hangar, Molly could hear Parker and Dwayne

revving up a machine. Somewhere behind them, Betsy and Penny courted a whole herd of goats, who'd discovered that Penny's heavy coat pockets were laden with goodies. She had everything from a bag of baby carrots to a half-eaten muffin, wrapped carefully in a paper towel.

Molly followed Liam inside. The structure was bigger on the inside than it had looked outside, and to her greater surprise, it wasn't a dirt floor with lofts of hay. It could have been an airplane hangar, if the Grangers were that type. Swept concrete floor spread across what had to be 3,000 square feet or more of open space. Unlike the red painted wood siding on the outside, the interior was plastered in clean white. Small square windows stood in pairs on each of the longer walls. Opposite the big, barn style doors, on the very farthest wall, there was a roll up gate. This is where the boys were—opening the gate and moving a Gator outside and casting fumes into the space.

"Hurry up, boys!" Liam called after them. "Get it out!"

"It's like a garage in here," Molly pointed out.

"That's right. We used to house all the equipment in here, but I sold off a bunch. Just keeping the basics now. The tractor. Gator and trailer. Baler."

"Sounds like a lot still." But Molly didn't spy the named machines in the hangar.

Liam said, "They're all outside now. The boys have a pretty good sense of what needs doing."

Molly had no idea what the boys might be up to, but she was coming to realize she didn't care. She'd much rather have Liam to herself during this supposed training session.

Besides the one Gator and a ride-on lawnmower, the only other substantial items in the space were stacks and stacks of long fold up tables and metal chairs, all neatly lined along the north facing wall.

Liam strode back a few steps and grabbed a clipboard that had been hanging inconspicuously from the wall by the door. He studied it in silence a moment.

"I haven't taken a look at this yet." Then, he peered outside as if searching for something. Or someone. When he returned his gaze to the clipboard, Molly thought she saw his eyes go wet, but he blinked and turned his head, gave a short cough, cleared his throat, and again looked at the board. "I guess my aunt went ahead and booked this year's vendors."

Molly nodded, as much as to assure herself that Liam was okay as to assure *him* that his aunt's forward motion was a good thing. Maybe it wasn't. Maybe this was all too soon for the poor rancher who lost his dad so suddenly and so, so terribly recently.

Part of her wanted to back out of the hangar, run to the minibus, and leave behind the agriculture program and the school, the kids, Liam, and the ocean of sadness churning behind his eyes.

Another part of Molly wanted to grab Liam's calloused hands and pull him into a long, deep hug. The kind of hug that would have them both crying and smiling and all warm and gooey inside when they finally released one another.

But that would be highly inappropriate. And anyway, Liam was still the reason Molly was here, at a ranch, instead of in her classroom, preparing a cooking lesson. He might not be a direct enemy, but he wasn't exactly a hero, either.

"Let's see," Liam said, his eyes—now clearly dry— tracing down a list. "Who else? Let's see. As usual, we have the logging outfitters here—it's a big company known well across town. Dempsey's the name. It used to belong to Mr. Griffin, but he retired. I thought they might have shut down, but I think the son runs it. Griffin. He's a bit older than us—" Liam indicated the two of them, and it made Molly's heart skip a beat, ridiculously. "I mean, I assume you're, what? Twenty...*two*?"

She flushed. "Twenty-*three*."

"I'm twenty-five."

Molly nodded and pushed down a ridiculously goofy smile that was trying hard to plaster itself up half her face.

"You're just a baby," Liam said.

At this, Molly glowered playfully. "You're two years older than me."

He shrugged. "I figured we were close in age."

"What gave it away?" She worried he was going to say it was the fact that she couldn't seem to hang on to the one teaching position she'd managed to get in her adult life. Of course, he wouldn't know that.

Instead he said, "Oh, lots of little things."

"Lots?" Molly stood a little taller. She propped her hands on her hips and shook her single braid from her shoulder to her back. "Like what?"

She watched in burning anticipation as Liam lowered the clipboard and gave her a long, soft look. At last, he said, "For starters, it's the way you dress."

"And how do I dress?"

He grinned. "Well, maybe not the way you dress, but the way you...undress?"

Molly froze, and when she looked at Liam, he was unfazed by what he'd said.

"Not like that." He shook his head and his boyish blonde hair fell over his forehead deliciously. He shook it back and grinned. "What I mean is it's the way you leave your clothes behind when you go to a stranger's house. That's not very wise of you, ya' know. What if I mistook them for belonging to some other girl? Then what?"

Molly felt her face turn red as a pepper. *Some other girl.* He was trying to get her riled up. She couldn't let him get away with that little dig. She had to fight back. "Maybe I just forgot which stranger's house I was in." She felt her throat close up. When did she get this brazen?

His light eyes glimmered like ice. "Really? You got me confused with some other guy?" He moved in even closer yet.

"You think you're special, huh?"

Liam shrugged again, and she could have sworn his body had closed in on hers.

She clasped her hands behind her back, fully aware what the movement did to bring her chest closer to his. Then Molly said, "So that's all you've got? You think I'm young because I left my clothes here. Clothes that your dog tore, I might add."

"I'll handle Georgie. And anyway, there are other clues."

"Oh?" They were back to square one, then.

He tapped his finger on his lower lip. "Your hair." The toes of his work boots kissed the toes of hers. They were far past the boundaries of decency now.

Molly felt his breath hot on her face. "My hair?" She swooped a hand behind her head and pulled her braid forward again, examining it like it held every answer to every question swirling in her mind. "What about my hair?" She looked back up, and his face was near enough to her forehead that his lips might brush it.

He grinned, and a pair of dimples formed on each of his cheeks. Had she noticed those before? "You've got those little baby hairs." He again reached over, daringly running the side of his thumb along her face by her ear.

"They're called flyaways. I can't help it."

"I love them."

Molly's chest clenched. Her pulse raced and heat crept up her neck. She felt herself sway forward into him, and in response, Liam edged closer. They were millimeters apart now, and when he dropped his hand from her face, it brushed along her arm.

Liam licked his lips.

Molly let her eyes close for a moment before she looked up at him. "Is that all?"

"Your eyes," he replied.

"What about my eyes?" She felt herself sway forward another half an inch.

Liam took the final step, and their bodies now touched. Molly's hands found Liam's, and they interlaced their fingers together at their sides. Her hips pressed against his, and her entire body was burning with excitement.

Liam frowned down at her. His Adam's apple bobbed as he swallowed, and he said in a low voice, "You have these...*great* big eyes and I swear I think I can see a million questions banked inside of them."

Her breath caught. "Maybe they aren't questions."

"Then what could they be?"

"Secrets."

"No." His tone confident, he shook his head assuredly. "You're not the type."

"I do have a secret." Her mouth was forming words that must have lived in her heart, but the whole experience was out-of-body, as though she was compelled not to think, but to act and to speak not from any place of logic, but from her heart alone.

"So do I," Liam whispered as he lowered his face to hers.

Molly found herself struggling to breathe. She couldn't speak to answer him. Couldn't make a sound if her life depended on it. Her voice was caught in her throat, exactly where her heart had lodged too. And, before she knew it, Liam's secret was Molly's and Molly's secret was Liam's and their lips were touching.

Chapter 22 — Liam

Whatever was happening—whatever was *going to happen*—between Liam and Molly was out of line. Inappropriate. It was too far. He felt disgrace course through his body. What would his dad think of Liam's behavior? Here he was, obligated to teach this girl a thing or two about ranching and farming, and he was taking advantage. Shame on Liam.

Other thoughts swelled in his brain, like how his dad had told him what was what when it came to women.

The late Larry Granger's words drifted into Liam's consciousness. *Easier that a heart goes hard than gets broken.*

Liam understood his dad's worry. If Liam were to ever find someone to love, he'd have to deal with the risk of losing her, just like Liam's mom had left them.

What if Molly was the sort to leave? Her family didn't live in Prairie Creek. Heck, Liam didn't even know if she had any family to speak of. He made a mental note to ask.

Anyhow, despite all these doubts, something else rang

true. Liam knew that whatever was growing between him and Molly Maison, it wasn't innately bad. Maybe he knew this because she was easy on the eyes or maybe because he saw in Molly the sort of woman his dad would have loved. Someone hard-working. Someone who was up for adventure. Someone willing to try something new, much like Larry Granger had done when he'd bought the ranch and made a go of what was a new lifestyle for him, at first.

Plus, Molly didn't deserve Liam's scorn or hard feelings. It wasn't *her* fault his mom left him when he was a baby. It wasn't Molly's fault, either, that she was assigned to Liam as a veritable student.

Then again, it *was* kind of Molly's fault that he was falling for her.

He couldn't stand it, and after too brief a moment, he dipped his head lower and slid each hand around her waist, pulling her into him.

But Molly grabbed Liam's wrists and pushed gently away. She opened her brown eyes and looked up at him, and he saw that despite her pushing, there wasn't a *no* in those eyes. She bit down on her lower lip. Liam's insides were all mush. He wished he could scoop Molly up right then and there and carry her into one of the back barns and lay her out on a checkered tablecloth and—

Molly whispered through parted lips, "That was…"

"That was wrong. I'm sorry," he finished her sentence as quickly as he could get the darn words out of his mouth.

"No, no." Her eyebrows crinkled in, and a small grin shaped her mouth like a little heart. "Not wrong, just—"

"Not appropriate." He smoothed his shirt down his torso and made a show of turning his expression very serious. "I'm sorry, Molly. Really, I shouldn't be taking advantage of you like this. You're here to help me, and I'm supposed to be helping you learn, and—"

"It's not like I'm listening to you," she pointed out.

He marveled at her quip. "Not listening to me? You're a bad student, then?"

"Maybe you're a bad teacher."

"You would know."

She grinned wider. "I'll try harder."

"Me too." He cleared his throat and rolled his shoulders back, putting on as intellectual a voice as he could muster. "As I was saying, class." He eyed her. "As far as vendors go, we also have Miles Gentry—there's another name you'll want to write down."

"I wasn't taking notes."

"You should. You should take this very seriously, Ms. Maison. Or should I say Molly?"

"Yessir," she replied, pouting her lips.

"That's right. Miles and his sister, Lucy, together with their folks run Gentry's Shoot 'n' Sport just out of town. It's a shooting range and hunting shop. They have a cousin who's a taxidermist, and so we ended up including a booth for him, too, as you can see."

Liam couldn't keep the act going. He broke character. "Have you met any of the Gentrys?"

"No. Doesn't ring a bell."

It occurred to Liam that maybe Molly hadn't made too many connections in town yet. "What about..." his voice trailed off momentarily as he examined the list on his clipboard. "Oh, here we go." He tapped a name. "You probably know the Ryersons. Mabel and Logan?"

"Ryersons." She squinted up at him. "I don't think so?"

"You said you sew, right?"

"Sew?" Alarm opened up over her face. "No. I said I *didn't* sew. That's why the sleeve fell out of my jacket."

"It wasn't...sewn on to begin with?"

"I thought I told you, I found that thing at The Thrifty Thistle."

"And they were selling it with assembly required?"

Molly burst into laughter, and Liam couldn't help but join. Not because his joke was funny but because Molly's entire affect was contagious.

There was no coming down from the high that was being with Molly Maison, but when they finally stopped laughing, Liam explained. "Mabel Ryerson runs The Thimble Shoppe. Maybe you've seen it."

"And her brother runs it with her?"

"Okay so *Logan* actually runs a motel thingy just outside of town. Or, I guess it's a bed and breakfast. It's sort of crazy, but he's got this celebrity there—"

Molly lit up at that. "Kelly Watts!"

Liam cocked his head. "Yeah."

"She has a YouTube channel. Or at least, she *did*. I've used some of her recipes. When I found out she was in Prairie Creek..."

Lifting an eyebrow, Liam prepared himself for a crazy story about how Molly moved to town just because she heard there had been glimpses of an internet celebrity there.

Instead, Molly said, with notable discomfort, "I almost didn't take the job at the high school."

"Why not?"

"I can't compete with the likes of Kelly Watts."

"How would you be competing with her?" Liam lowered the clipboard. "She's not a teacher."

"I mean, I don't know. Nobody knows what she's doing these days. What if she's still putting out content? And if so, what if I use one of her recipes? Locally? And like...she finds out?"

"Wouldn't that be the point? For her recipes to get out to the world?"

"What if I do a bad job of it?"

A lightbulb clicked for Liam. Molly figured the school board pulled the rug on the culinary program because she was a bad Culinary Arts teacher.

When, in fact, this town didn't know salmon from sushi. And also, the reality had nothing to do with the school at all, really. It was a runaway train.

Could Liam just come out and say that the whole mess was his aunt's fault? She was the one who opened the floodgates of discontent and stoked the fires of locals who saw themselves as old-timey farmers? Farmers who needed teenage boys to work the fields? And even though it was Betsy who maybe started it, the truth was that Creek folk simply didn't see the value in paying an extra $25 so their kids could learn to soufflé. They needed it—they needed a taste of the world, but they just didn't know it.

Molly could teach them. "The high school, heck, Molly, the *town* needs you. And not as a ranch hand or whatever they're trying to make you out to be."

Her face did a funny thing—her mouth screwed into a quizzical knot. "What are you saying?"

Now, Liam might not be the sharpest knife in the drawer, but he knew when he'd stepped into a lobster trap.

He thought very carefully about what he was going to say next. Then, after a long moment, he answered, "I'm saying..." he licked his lips. "I'm saying I'm probably the luckiest person in Prairie Creek, South Dakota."

"What do you mean?"

The heat between them hadn't left even when they turned their kiss into a playful resistance movement and even when that turned into a study of Molly's self-doubt. But here it was, raging back to life in earnest. It was all Liam could do not to grab her by the waist and carry her to a back barn and throw her into a pile of hay and—

"There you are!" Betsy Granger's voice rang like an alarm behind them.

Liam fell back a full stride, nearly tripping, and Molly twisted away, hiding her blushing face and trembling lips.

Betsy and Penny burst into the hangar side by side. Betsy held a pile of something in her arms and wore a look of horror. Penny, however, looked delighted.

"Hi, Bets. Hey Penny. We are just going over the vendors' list." He rapped the clipboard with his knuckles. "Fully booked, it looks like." He slid a glance to Molly who chewed her lower lip adorably. Her big brown eyes looked bigger. *Caught in the act*. Almost.

Betsy eyed Liam.

Penny folded her arms and looked on the verge of something. "Caught ya!" She pointed a finger at Liam and Molly, but he had no idea why.

Chapter 23 — Molly

Molly eyed Penny with a warning look. She knew exactly what was happening, and she knew she'd ward it off easily and quickly. She had to. Not only because Molly couldn't handle any weirdness or rumors, but because Molly wanted something else entirely.

She wanted the world to stop so she and Liam could abscond together somewhere private. But here was her student and Liam's aunt, and the latter was carrying Molly's clothes.

Liam wasn't as quick on the uptake, and when Molly stole a glance his way, she saw confusion colored his features.

Molly wasn't confused though. "Oh, that's nothing," she started, ready with a simple explanation. Before she could give it, though, the same door through which Betsy and Penny had entered burst open a second time. Dwayne and Parker were in tears from laughter. Parker whooped in the air. Dwayne made a funnel with his hands and belted a low, "*Grangerrrr!*"

Molly froze. What was this? While Liam did nothing more than push a hand through his hair, Betsy stared ice daggers at the two of them, Penny giggled, and the boys made animalistic sounds, Molly froze.

Finally, she stammered, "I fell. When I was here, I fell, spilled hot cocoa and had to change."

"Suuuurrre," Parker dragged the word out inanely.

Molly looked to Liam for help, but he too appeared frozen. "Liam, tell them," she prompted.

Quickly, he wiped the grin off his face and stepped up to Molly, taking her side. Before Liam could say one word, though, Dwayne whipped out his phone and held it up, filming everything that happened next.

Chapter 24 — Liam

L iam only cared about one thing, the truth. And the truth was, though Molly's clothes weren't indicative of anything improper, he *was* falling for her.

What was so wrong with that?

"She changed her clothes in my bathroom," Liam explained to the gawking face of his aunt and the leering faces of the three kids.

Penny asked, "And she left her clothes here?"

"It was late," Molly offered, but Liam quickly saw in her eyes that it wasn't what she wanted to say. It gave the wrong impression.

So, he added, "We were working. She came in and we had supper together."

"Together?" Betsy raised an eyebrow.

"What did she change *into*?" Parker asked.

Liam scowled at the brat. "An extra pair of clothes. What else?" Then, Liam pointed a finger at Dwayne and his phone. "Put that down. This isn't a viral video." Dwayne slowly lowered the device but kept it out. Liam didn't have time for teenage pranks. "Listen, nothing *happened*. Trust me. I wish it *had*."

It was the wrong thing to say. The *very* wrong thing because right as the words had flown from Liam's mouth, Molly's eyes flashed at him. "I have to go," she half-whispered.

And then, she was gone.

Chapter 25 — Molly

Time swallowed the week whole. Soon enough, it was the weekend, and Molly didn't know what to do with herself. After the humiliation of being present in the moment of discovery, things had gotten worse.

Kids took to the school days with a new vim and vigor, making crude jokes in hushed voices and feeding the machine of small town gossip.

Come Friday, even Mr. Porter wanted a word with the now infamous Molly Maison.

He'd asked her what happened, to which she'd been painfully honest. It wasn't what it had looked like, she assured him. But, yes, there were feelings forming between Molly and her mentor.

Mr. Porter hadn't been unreasonably upset, going so far as to say that he understood how *these things can happen*. He'd even remarked what a nice match the pair would make, much to Molly's further mortification. Ultimately, however, he'd suggested that they carry on with the training and plans and that he'd talk to Liam about the responsibility he owned in taking Molly on at the ranch. She hated that as much or more than if it'd been her fault. Molly wasn't chattel, and she wasn't a victim, either. She and Liam had shared a kiss in mutual consent. They were adults. They were—

Molly didn't know what they were. Or where she fit in Prairie Creek. The whole thing had resulted in a personal crisis, in fact. So much so, that while she agreed to continue to help and learn, she privately started to make other plans.

And all the while Molly was making other plans, she was longing for Liam. Thinking of him. Fantasizing about him. And hating him too. He was the reason for her heartache. For her crisis. For her crushed dreams. She was more certain of that than ever. Especially when days went by without a single text or phone call from Liam.

Now, Molly had to commit to protecting not only her career, but her heart too.

Naturally, there was only one place for a girl to turn when her heart was in danger, home. Home to Molly was up in the air, so she picked the next best thing, her mom.

Molly called Jean Maison first thing Saturday morning. After Molly rehashed just about everything, Jean had one thing to say. "Do you know the story of your dad and me?"

"What do you mean?" Molly asked, equal parts deflated from spilling her guts and intrigued to hear more about where she came from. "Like, you and dad...how you started dating?"

"It was in Mimi's restaurant and bakery in Aberdeen.

Le Cœur. I wanted a job waiting tables. Your dad washed dishes."

"How old were you two?"

"Not very." Jean laughed. "He was twenty. I was nineteen."

"Love at first sight?"

"Lust." Her mom's voice went airy.

Molly shifted uncomfortably. Maybe she *didn't* want to hear this. "*Mom*," she groaned.

"You know what? We wouldn't have met or had you if it weren't for Mimi. She hired me on the spot and sent me back to grab an apron and ice cakes."

"She had that much faith in you just from your first impression?"

Jean laughed again. "I think it was a ploy. Later, Mimi told me she was sorry to have set us up, your dad and me. If she had known the type of boy she raised, she'd never have put me through it." Jean paused. "But I don't see it that way."

"Why not? Dad left us."

"He didn't stick around, but without your dad, I wouldn't have had *you*, Molly."

Molly could roll her eyes at the corniness, or she could accept this as the truth. "You're saying it all worked out for the best?"

"Yep. That's what I'm saying."

"Don't you wish you'd...applied somewhere else? Or that you'd quit before things got too far? Or maybe even that you never married him to begin with? You could have had me without the headache of a man."

"Then I wouldn't have had Mimi, either. I wouldn't have saved up enough money to see me through college to get a job. I wouldn't have had someone to watch you and help raise you. Everything *worked out*, Molly."

Molly was glad to hear of all this, but...something still niggled in the back of her brain. "Mom?"

"Yeah?"

"You say that applying for a job at the bakery was your destiny. Right?"

"In a way."

"Well, what if my destiny is to leave Prairie Creek? What if my destiny was never Prairie Creek or—"

"What about Penny?"

"Huh?"

"Your student, Penny. And her brother—what's his name?"

"Parker. Parker Porter. He's a real pill, but I like him fine. Yeah. Dwayne on the other hand, he's the one who filmed this whole thing and shared it out. They even suspended him."

"That's good."

"Yeah, but it was too late. Kids had seen it. They talked about me, sometimes right in front of my face."

"And Betsy?"

"What about her?"

"You like her."

"She's judgy."

"Judgy can be good. We all need a little accountability."

"I can find a judgy aunt anywhere."

"And Liam?"

"What about him?"

"You like him. A lot, Molly."

"What is it you always tell me? There are plenty of fish in the sea."

"Is that your excuse then? He's just a fish? One of many?"

"This isn't about Liam. This is about me. And anyway —" Molly remembered the coldest truth of them all. "He hasn't even called. Not since this all happened."

"All right."

"All right?" Molly was indignant. She made a quick left turn in the conversation, unreasonably angry with her mother and, truthfully, with herself. "I guess the real reason I called was to see if you were coming down, Mom. For Thanksgiving."

"Will you still be there?"

"*Yes.*" Petulant, Molly added, "I'm staying on through the year."

"Ah. So you have time, then."

"Time for what?"

"To see what happens."

Her mother's calm demeanor could really drive Molly right up the wall. "See you on Thursday then."

"I'll see you then."

Molly got off the phone, and when she did, she jumped onto her computer and pulled up a million tabs. Everything from comfort recipes to the news to her favorite music app to, finally, a webpage for Brown County Schools.

With the pointless anger having nowhere to go, she made a rash decision. One that would let her take out her frustration somewhere. Molly opened the Careers tab, scrolled to Open Positions, then brought up the electronic application.

Then, Molly Maison applied for a job somewhere else. Away from Prairie Creek. Penny. Betsy. Away from Liam and his homestead.

Chapter 26 — Liam

The week felt long but the weekend felt longer yet. Liam was nearly ready for the festival, and so come Sunday, Liam was itching for Monday. Especially since it was the next time he was sure to see Molly.

Phil Porter had called Liam the day after Molly had stormed out of the hangar. He had said whatever happened was their business. He was pleased to know Molly was making *friends*, but when it came to the school setting and Molly and Liam's connections to the students, it was Liam's obligation to set an example.

At first, Liam hadn't understood. Nothing *happened*, he'd assured Phil.

That was when Phil had pulled the trump card. "Son, if your dad was here, he'd say the same thing. Flaunting an illicit affair with a young teacher is no way to behave."

At that, Liam had seethed. *Seethed*. Firstly, there was no *illicit affair*. Secondly, Phil's invocation of the late Larry

Granger and his morals and ideals was way out of line. Liam had even said so. Standing up to Phil Porter, however, was clearly unheard of. Phil hadn't taken kindly to Liam calling him out on overstepping his boundaries in chastising not only Liam but also the breath of fresh air that was Molly.

Then came in Betsy, who had another take on things. She'd shamed Liam at first too. But by the time he'd explained and reexplained himself, she came around.

Even so, the whole mess really bugged Liam. Molly had run away as if it were true. Not only as if it were true, but they acted like it was the year 1800, and everyone had come together to fasten a red A on her shirt.

Every night that passed, Liam picked up his phone to call. And every night, he thought better of it. Something inside was telling him to give her space. Give her time. Let her come back to him. It was only two days of that thinking before Liam couldn't take it anymore.

He'd gone so far as to bring up Molly's phone number on his cell, when a thought struck him down like lightning. Could he get her in trouble? What was Phil saying to Molly? What were the kids saying at the high school?

Maybe this really *was* more serious than Liam knew. After all, Liam didn't know the first thing about the world of a school and its charges. Maybe parents were up in arms.

So, instead of calling Molly, he called his aunt for some wisdom.

She'd come over right away.

Right away ended up not being until Sunday for supper. Thursday early morning, Betsy had been called out to Wisconsin to see about an auction she and Liam had already discussed attending. It had been slated for the following week, but with a storm in the forecast, they moved the plans. Instead of both going, it was agreed Liam would stay with the students and continue prep for the festival and Betsy would represent the ranch.

She had to go too. If they wanted to keep the ranch profitable and working, which...they were. Especially with the latest movements between the school district and the ranch.

"I am *so* sorry, Liam Lawrence!" Betsy fell into the front door on a blustery wind. "That storm was hot on our heels the whole time I was out there. Praise be that I could make it here before nightfall, anyhow. Ugh!"

She was buried deep in layers and layers, and by the time she'd unwrapped herself, like a mummy, Liam had set the table and served them.

Betsy's presence seemed to annoy Georgie who slinked from the kitchen and holed up on his chair in the living room.

Betsy joined Liam at the table and poured herself a generous glass of red wine and tipped the bottle to Liam, who shook his head.

With drinks decided and the plates full, the lonesome duo tucked into ribs, mac 'n' cheese, mashed taters, and steamed carrots. Liam had found the recipe from that homestead lady who lived local.

By the time they'd buttered their rolls, Georgie wandered back in too. He was annoyed, but not so annoyed as to miss a chance at scraps.

"Well?" Betsy poked at him with her fork over a pile of

ribs on her plate. Betsy was the type of woman to make eating a chore. She didn't start right away, and she asked questions every time Liam took a great big bite of his food. "How is it all going?"

He chewed laboriously.

"Take your time." Betsy had every chance to take her own great big bite, but instead she swigged from her glass and made baby noises at Georgie, who skittered beneath the table. "Now," Betsy declared. "As for *Molly*. I've done a little digging." She made a show of scooping up a great pile of mashed potatoes and laughing at her own joke.

"Digging? What do you mean?" Liam eyed her through another bite of ribs.

"Actually, before we get to Molly Maison..." She put her spoon down and lifted a paper towel to her lips, dabbing them with a purpose and frowning at her plate. "Liam, there's something needs talking over." She pinned him with a pained look.

Liam swallowed the last of his bite. He said, "Okay?"

"It's your daddy, Liam."

Liam stifled a groan. His fork, piled high in mashed potatoes, hovered just beyond the reach of his lips. "What of him?" He knew he was being sharp with her, but he couldn't help it.

"Liam, it's not every day a boy loses his father. You're hurting. I know."

She didn't. Was it also not every day that a boy lost both his parents and had to suffer regular inquiries from his aunt? He kept his mouth shut on that particular question.

"Liam," Betsy went on. "When are we going to...*you*

know?" She narrowed her eyes to slits and made a frowning mouth and nodded her head in what was meant to be an encouraging way.

He set his fork down without taking the bite. This wasn't the first time Betsy had brought up the hope chest. That's how he knew what she was talking about. Whenever Betsy mentioned Larry, it was always about Larry's bedroom, his clothes, and that old chest. As if going through Larry's things held some magical answer to some magical question. But how could they? Any answers Liam had ever needed in life had died right along with his dad. "No. No interest."

"Hon." She balked. "No *interest*?" She squinted harder. "Liam, hon. We have to go through your dad's stuff. How about tonight? Get it over with?"

"Get it over with?" Liam picked up his fork and shoved the potatoes into his mouth then plucked a shard of meat from a rib and passed it down to Georgie as if it might be a great comeback to Betsy.

"Oh, honey, that's *not* what I meant. Not at all." Betsy reached across the table and gripped Liam's clenched fist. "I'll do it with you. It's *time*, Liam."

"Time to get rid of him for good?" Liam's voice choked.

"Time for *you* to have a new chapter. Start fresh. Clean house a little. Just because we toss out a few t-shirts doesn't mean you're getting rid of your dad. He'd tell you the same thing."

She was right, and he knew it. That didn't make the truth easier to stomach.

He grumbled a reluctant, "Fine," and stabbed his fork

into the mac 'n' cheese. "After supper." Anyway, he had a feeling she wouldn't discuss Molly with him unless he gave in.

Betsy beamed. "Now, hon. What was it you wanted to talk to *me* about?"

Chapter 27 — Liam

"Molly," Liam announced.

"Oh." Betsy's spoon nearly clattered to the plate. She was quick to dab her lips and lace her fingers, propping her elbows on the top of the table and leaning toward Liam. "Of course, hon. Whatever you two did—it's positively no one's business but your *own*." She winked at him.

Liam fumed. "Betsy, we didn't *do* anything. And despite that, Mr. Porter has made this huge fuss over it and how she and I need to set an example for the kids and—"

"Well, you *do*," Betsy said pointedly.

He lowered his own fork. "You think I should back off of her then?"

Betsy's eyes flashed. "So you *are* seeing each other?"

"No, we're...we like each other." This was beyond painful. Liam took a deep breath. "I like her. I think she likes me, but ever since the..."

"The scandal," Betsy offered helpfully.

Liam frowned. "The *non*-scandal, yes. Ever since then, she hasn't texted, called or showed up here."

"Well I'm sure Phil is prickly about it. I mean she's on the clock, in a way when she's here."

"And whose fault is that?" Liam hadn't meant to come down hard on his aunt, but once again—if she hadn't stuck her nose in all of this then... well, then Liam may never have gotten to know Molly Maison. His anger began to dissipate. "Sorry, Aunt Bets."

"No. No. I guess I'm not being much help."

"I don't necessarily need any help; I just really like her." He couldn't believe he was admitting all of this to Betsy just now. And yet it felt just about as important as anything else. Even as important as going through his dad's stuff.

Betsy picked up her fork and knife and sawed into the ribs, which didn't need any sawing. Meat fell from the bone and she scooped it up with her fork, then chewed thought-fully. "Hon, I don't think you need any help at all. I don't actually know why you're asking me."

"I mean I'm asking you if I should contact her."

"Wait a minute, wait a minute, you haven't tried to?"

"I told you no. Mr. Porter warned me off of her. I don't know if he said the same to her, but she hasn't contacted me, either."

"It's an impasse." Fire lit up Betsy's eyes. "An impasse."

"Okay?" He was more confused now. "So?"

"It demands action."

"From me?"

"From whoever wants it more."

"Do I want it more?"

Betsy pressed her lips in a firm line.

Point taken. "I'll call her as soon as we're done," he promised to himself more than to Betsy.

* * *

They finished supper speedily, and with great reluctance, Liam followed Betsy to the far back bedroom of the cabin. Behind Liam, Georgie followed too. A little less reluctantly, Liam noted.

"Here we are." Betsy took in a deep breath. "Wow. Smells just like him."

Tears burned hot in Liam's throat. He tried to cough but instead, a sob came out.

Betsy shot across the room to him, sweeping his tall form into her small embrace. She felt strong to him. Like she could carry his grief on her shoulders. Liam wondered if that's where he might put it. At least for a little while. At least while he did this terrible chore.

An hour of crying and sorting later, and they'd made their way through Larry's dresser drawers, his closet, and a small bedside table where he kept the Bible and his only set of reading glasses. Larry Granger wasn't one to have backups.

But Liam knew there was still one more thing. The chest that sat neatly at the end of his own bed in his bedroom. The one Georgie slept atop. The one Liam had sat on and cried on in the days after his dad's death.

"The chest," he grumbled to his aunt. "I'll handle it later."

"Let's do it now. Maybe there's something you need."

"What would I need?" he asked Betsy. "Everything is

done. Dad's buried. His will is done." Indeed, Larry's will had been easy enough. The acreage they owned went into a trust. The cabin and the acre upon which it sat went right into Liam's name. The cottage and the half acre on which it sat went right into Betsy's name. If ever there came a time that Liam or Betsy wanted to sell the rest of the land, they'd have to go through the trust. Everything else was to be divvied out according to the wishes of Liam and Betsy.

There was no one else who would have a claim to anything.

No one except for Sharla Granger. When Liam had brought up that point in the estate meeting with the lawyer, though, Betsy had cleared her throat and promised him that Sharla was a moot point.

Liam recalled Betsy exchanging a look with the lawyer. He'd chalked it up to family shame, pure and simple.

"You never know. Maybe your dad had a...maybe there are family photos in there. Ones of your mom?"

Liam shook his head sourly, but even so he said, "I'll go through it on my own, then."

Betsy squeezed his shoulder. "If you change your mind. I'll help. Okay?"

He nodded.

Once she'd gone, Liam gave a short, low whistle. On command, Georgic followed him back to his own bedroom.

As if the pooch understood, he stayed off the chest and instead, sat at attention beside Liam, who lowered into a squat next to the heavy wooden box.

One hand made its way to the far latch, pushing the hook out. With his left hand, Liam did the same on the other side. There were no locks on the chest, and that alone should tell Liam he'd find no surprises inside.

As if an answer appeared plainly in front of him, Liam stopped short of opening the lid.

Georgie yelped at the box, though. *Go on, Dad. Do it!*

If Liam opened the chest, what would he find? His grandpa's pipe? His grandmother's afghan? That was probably the best-case scenario. Worst case, he'd find...oh, who knew? Paperwork indicating there were heart issues? Medical results that could have warned Liam? Something else entirely that he wasn't ready for? Like the whereabouts of Liam's mom—which he didn't care to know?

The only thing that any new knowledge could bring was a distraction.

Liam latched up both sides and pulled the heavy wool blanket back over the chest.

Whatever was inside could wait.

Liam had other fish to fry. Namely, a phone call.

Chapter 28 — Molly

Sunday night saw Molly soaking in the tub. She had a long week ahead of her. A week of work and a week of seeing Liam every night. If she was still welcome. Mr. Porter had emailed her to say it was a good idea to get back to the ranch come Monday. So long as she and Liam behaved themselves.

His admonishment was uncomfortable at the least and enraging at the worst. She wasn't a child. If she was in trouble with her boss, that was one thing. But to warn her off of her own personal attachments?

That was the problem with falling for someone at *work*, Molly realized as she sank to chin-level in her bathtub. Then, she sat up straight, splashing water out onto the floor. *Falling* for someone? Was she *falling* for Liam Granger?

Hardly.

She sank back below the waterline, submerged her entire body from head to toe. She stayed under the water holding her breath. When she couldn't stand it another moment, she launched herself upwards and faced reality. Molly was positively falling for Liam Granger. She was head over heels infatuated. She loved the way he looked. She loved what he did for work and where he lived. She loved his heartache, which was twisted she knew, but it made him just enough vulnerable that he wasn't perfect, and Molly didn't want perfect. She wanted Liam.

But he didn't want her. Because if he did, he'd have called. She couldn't risk her reputation any further. She wasn't going to fall for him.

Molly had to push her desires out of her mind. Her entire future depended on it. Anyway, where could things with Liam possibly go? Her prospects in Prairie Creek were shot to hay now. The best she could hope for was keeping her job as an agriculture teacher, and Molly didn't teach ag. She taught cooking. Maybe not well. Not yet, anyway, but cooking was her world. Her heart. Her *legacy*.

Memories in Mimi's kitchen swirled in Molly's head as her fingers and toes pruned. She remembered the first time she learned to make cinnamon apple Bostock. She remembered when she botched an entire batch of chocolate soufflé only for Mimi to laugh and throw her hands up and say, *nothing is ever ruined, mon amor.*

Amazingly, Molly could recall her retort like it was yesterday. *Yes, Mimi, I've wasted all of this.*

Wasted what? How? Absurdité!

With that, Mimi had swatted Molly with a dishtowel. *Molly Maison*, Mimi had hissed then took a spoon and stabbed at the brown heap, shoveled it into her mouth and pretended to melt on the floor. When Mimi had recovered from her pretend faint and Molly had recovered from the giggles, Mimi had added this pearl. *Even if you have all the right ingredients and you follow the recipe, things can turn out much differently than you wanted. This, Molly Maison, is not a waste.*

Molly had asked, *then what is it?*

Mimi had grinned and scooped another spoonful of the lumpy chocolate dessert. *A delicious mess.*

A *delicious mess.* Is that what Molly had gotten herself into now? Her brain screamed that she'd somewhere gone wrong and now everything was ruined. But below, in the deep recesses of her chest where her heart beat, she knew that Mimi was right. Nothing was wasted. It just hadn't turned out quite right. Maybe Molly had to come to Prairie Creek to learn about where her fresh ingredients came from? That was something, wasn't it?

And besides, maybe she needed a detour on her way to an even better Culinary Arts teaching position. Maybe all of this was going to lead her off the broken road and into a beautiful shiny kitchen back up in Aberdeen. There she'd finally find an apartment she could afford on a teacher's salary, rejoin her mom, and return home for good.

Except...

In just a few short months, Prairie Creek was beginning to feel a lot like home to her. And the people in it, even Mr. Porter, like family.

More confused than ever, Molly tried to put everything out of her mind. She headed to her bedroom, where she put on the cooking network and tucked herself deep into flannel sheets.

First, she suffered the news and weather forecast. Looking ahead to the week, the weather was to take a dip with a chance of early snowfall coming over the plains on Wednesday. If it did snow, that wouldn't necessarily change plans for the festival, but it might change plans for Molly's wardrobe. She'd planned each outfit meticulously, from Monday's farmer John overalls all the way to Friday's wool turtleneck dress with thick stockings and knee-high brown boots. She'd even selected her apron. The one that had belonged to Mimi, a cornflower blue with white paisley printed over it. The lace trim was probably once bright white but after so many decades had softened to the color of creamy milk. Stains peppered the fabric, but with so many—everything from carrot juice to radish stew to rhubarb jam—they added to the garment rather than detracting from it.

Molly watched TV distractedly. At her bedside table, her phone screen lit up.

She pulled it from its charging cable and squinted at the bright screen. A text notification had popped up.

Who would be texting so late on Sunday? She hoped it wasn't Mr. Porter. She could see it now. *Bad news, Ms. Maison—the school cannot support you hosting a table at the festival. In fact, your services are no longer needed at all. You don't even need to show up to school tomorrow. We've hired somebody else!*

Her gut clenched as she tapped her screen to see who it was that was messaging her and what he or she had to say.

Chapter 29 — Liam

Liam lay on top of his bed covers. At his feet, Georgie snored on the chest.

Normally, Liam would lie awake on his bed for hours before sleep would come. But today, after going through his dad's bedroom and coming to something akin to acceptance, Liam was feeling especially wired. He was going to call Molly. He was going to bare his soul to her. His heart. And he didn't have a single clue how to do that.

Even so, this wasn't up for debate. Liam was going to call Molly. Her number was programmed into his phone back from when she first started. All he had to do was tap her name and hit Call. Apologize for what he'd done. Beg her forgiveness if he had to. And, ultimately, tell her exactly how he felt—their professional arrangement be darned.

Finally ready, Liam reached across his bed to his nightstand. His hand fumbled in the dark across the wood tabletop, hitting the alarm clock and lamp.

His phone wasn't there. He reached down into each pocket of his sweats.

Nothing.

In the day to day, Liam didn't bring his phone anywhere with him. Since his dad's death, he associated it with bad news. Even though Liam wasn't one to give much credence to the notion of traumatic triggers, if pressed, he'd probably admit that getting phone calls sparked in him a great anxiety.

As such, Liam hadn't the first clue where the device might even be.

He sat up in bed. Georgie snorted awake and lifted his head. One ear lopped forward and the other backward. To emphasize his goofiness, he cocked his head and the backward flopped ear flipped over his head.

Liam smiled and asked his shaggy companion, "Where's my phone, Georgie?"

Georgie barked excitedly and jumped up onto the bed.

"Phone!" Liam commanded. Georgie bounded off the bed, tail and tongue wagging. Soon enough the pair were off on a hunt. Liam checked the whole cabin from his bedside table to the fridge.

He returned to his bedroom again and eyed the chest. There was no way his phone was in there, but he felt that urgent need creeping in again. Then, Georgie jumped up at the bedroom window and barked.

Liam followed the dog's pointing schnoz out into the brittle November night.

Sure enough, like a lighthouse for a sailor, the coach lights outside of the hangar shone, beckoning Liam and Georgie both to her safety.

Liam hurriedly pulled on his coat and stuffed his feet

into boots before stamping outside and around the porch to the hangar with Georgie hot on his heels.

He hauled open the door and flipped the lights on. Rows of overhead fluorescent lighting flickered to life, glowing down on two long rows of foldout tables, each with a sign taped to it indicating which vendor was assigned where.

Sure enough, Liam found his phone on top of his clipboard on the first table on the right—Molly Maison's table. Liam lingered momentarily as he tapped his phone back to life. The battery was at just 5%.

He stole a look at Georgie, who whined on the floor at his feet. "Here goes nothing."

Chapter 30 — Molly

It took her eyes a moment to adjust to what she was seeing, but once Molly realized the phone number belonged to Liam, her heart raced.

Why was he calling her so late on a Sunday night?

Was it *even* that late?

And, lastly, what did this really mean?

Her eyes traced over his name again in a flash. She hit Accept.

"Hello?"

"Hi, Molly? This is Liam Granger."

It was cute how he added his last name. As if she knew any other Liam and especially any other Liam Granger.

"Hi, Liam." She hesitated a split second. "Is everything okay?"

"I'm so sorry to bother you on a Sunday night. Is now a bad time?"

Her anxiety raged anew. "No! I'm up. It's no problem!"

Molly's heart raced and she sat up higher in bed, then

put her show on mute. This was important. She clutched the phone to her ear as she waited for Liam's response.

"Oh, whew." He laughed on the other end of the line.

Molly laughed, too, though at what she wasn't sure. "I'm just in bed. I mean...not like, *asleep*. I just got out of the bathtub." Ooh. Too much information.

Sure enough, Liam's voice turned husky. "Oh. The bath."

Molly wondered if her subconscious was taking over and giving him these improper details to lure him back to her. Then again, if she were trying to lure him back to her, it would mean she'd lost him. She never had him to begin with. And after a week of no contact, could it be said they were ever together? No, of course they weren't. They shared one kiss. One hot moment of romance that was more than likely a blip on his radar. "I take a bath every Sunday." She laughed again, nervous. Her pulse raced.

"Sounds relaxing."

"Yeah." She squeezed her eyes shut and bit down hard on her lower lip. She could die. "Um. So, how are you?"

"Oh, yeah. I'm sorry. Listen, um. About, um. About *everything*."

"About everything?" Where was this going. Stupid bath comment. Stupid bed comment. Stupid kiss! Ugh!

"I mean the, uh, the whole thing, yeah. In the hangar. If I embarrassed you or caused any problems. I'm *really* sorry."

"I'm not embarrassed." Lie.

"Oh. No, I didn't think you were. I just. It's just that Mr. Porter gave me a good talking to, and—"

"He did?" Molly's heart leapt.

"Yeah. I guess I was embarrassed," Liam admitted.

"You *were*?" Her heart sank.

"Not like that," he added quickly. "Molly, I... Listen. I know it's soon and we don't know each other well or anything, but, Molly, I really like you."

"You *do*?" She could hear a crackle over the line. Like he was shifting positions in his own bed. Then, a yip in the background. Georgie. Molly's heart found a consistent, if quick, rhythm. "Liam, I like you too." She shouldn't be saying this. Not after everything that happened. But then, it was the truth, and Molly was an honest person if nothing else.

"Whatever Phil says or however my aunt acts, can we just ignore that? Can we sort of tune everyone out and, I don't know, start over?"

"Start over?" Molly's pulse sped up again. "Like *all* the way over, or?"

"Well, not all the way over. I'd like to *not* forget that kiss."

Molly felt herself burn hot from the inside out. She kicked off her covers. New energy throbbed up her body. She couldn't just sit in bed and talk. She needed to move. Pace. Cook, even.

Whenever Molly got edgy or anxious, all she had to do to quell the nerves was to pull out her mimi's cookbook and thumb through it until she found something simple but yummy. Between the butter and whisking, it grounded her.

"What are you doing for Thanksgiving?" Liam asked suddenly.

"Oh, you mean besides baking a million pies for the festival?"

Again, static crackled over the line. Liam laughed and said, "Right. Besides that."

"My mom is coming to town. She lives in Aberdeen and I convinced her to come join me so I wasn't totally alone."

"Do you already have a turkey?"

"I bought one last week. It's thawing in my fridge. Why, do *you*?"

"We'll probably just do chicken."

"But it's Thanksgiving," she protested good-naturedly as she opened the fridge and withdrew a bowl of eggs and a stick of butter. Then, Molly swiveled to the counter and pulled the flour and sugar from the corner. She opened a cupboard and took out baking soda, baking powder, and brown sugar. She wasn't sure what she'd make. Maybe Beignets? Profiteroles? She'd need other ingredients. Tapping a finger on her lip she asked Liam distractedly, "Did you forget to get a turkey?"

"Naw. We just have excess chickens at the moment."

"Oh no." Molly giggled. "You really do live off the land. How could I have forgotten?"

"Maybe because you haven't been here in several days. Almost a week, to be exact."

"Well, you've never been here." Why did she say that? What was she implying?

"You live off of Main Street, right? In town?"

"In a little second floor apartment. I rent a room from Mrs. Zick." She thumbed through the cookbook until a recipe for Palmiers appeared. Also called elephant ears, it was a simple pastry that took on the shape of a heart. Molly felt it was perfect. Plus, she had store bought puff pastry in the fridge.

"I know Mrs. Zick," Liam offered. "We used to deliver fresh produce to her back when my dad was around."

"Why did you stop?"

"A lot of things stopped when he died."

Molly knew there was more to what Liam was implying. And she knew there was just one response to Liam now. "Maybe you could start again. Maybe tonight."

"I don't have any fresh produce. I don't think."

"You have jams, though. If I know my landlady, I think she wouldn't mind a Sunday evening call, especially if you arrived bearing treats."

"I think I'd need more of a reason than to just show up with a jar of jam and an awkward hello."

Molly returned coyly, "Don't you already have one?"

But instead of a reply, the air on the other end of the phone sounded suddenly muted. Had Molly said something wrong? Done something wrong? Overstepped? She checked the clock on the stove. It was half past eight. Not late but not early. Mrs. Zick was probably asleep. "Um, *Liam*?" she asked into the abyss of the cell phone line.

No answer came. Had he hung up? "Liam?" she said once again then pulled the phone away from her face to see the call had ended.

She had no idea why.

Chapter 31 — Liam

Liam wanted to slam his phone into the hardwood floor and stamp it out. He should have plugged it in as he was talking, but instead, he paced his cabin with Georgie underfoot. Right up until his phone died.

But even once it died, he'd had his answer.

Molly liked him back.

"Georgie, *thank you*." Giddy with excitement, Liam shucked his sweats and t-shirt for jeans and a flannel, his work boots, and a quick splash of water on his face. He added cologne he'd found from some random gift pack ages ago, brushed his teeth, and raked his hands through his hair. Then, when he was ready, he gave himself a good look in the mirror. At last, Liam scruffed Georgie around the neck, bopped his nose, and ducked with jacket in tow out to his truck.

It was only once Liam was rolling onto Main Street that an important oversight occurred to him.

Was this for real? Had Molly actually invited him over

late on this random Sunday night, and was Liam actually accepting the invitation and driving, relatively unannounced, into town to show up at Mrs. Zick's house, likely to startle the poor old woman?

He threw the truck into park outside the tall, white farmhouse. Most houses in Prairie Creek had once belonged to farms only later to have their parcels cut up and sold off. Mrs. Zick's was an original farmhouse on a reduced plat of land.

From the street outside, Liam could see two things clearly. His breath, quick and hot in the frigid night air, and a light on in a second story window above. Because Liam still wasn't thinking clearly, he hadn't brought his phone and charger or made any preparations for showing up. He'd just acted. Rashly, mind you.

But so long as Molly was being truthful, then he'd be welcome. And if she wasn't, then it was just as well he learn so now.

Liam's heart pounded inside his chest.

Chapter 32 — Molly

M olly didn't stop at popping Palmiers into the oven, oh no. She'd decided upon a full spread. If Liam hadn't just hung up and if he did appear, he'd be cold and hungry, no doubt. And if he *had* hung up and didn't appear, she'd have a complete supper and carry some downstairs to Mrs. Zick, who probably could use a hearty midwestern meal.

After the pastry was molded and sugared and cooking to a warm buttery brown, she pulled out a fresh set of chicken cutlets, which she set about seasoning and marinating at a leisurely pace. Once they were soaking in an olive oil-lemon mixture, she turned back to her fridge, rummaging inside until she emerged with carrots. Perfect. More seasoning and marinating and then Molly added red potatoes and after more seasoning still, she put together a skillet to include the cutlets and vegetables and set it to simmer on the stovetop.

It had been a solid twenty minutes since her phone call

with Liam had abruptly ended, and it was beginning to settle into Molly's mind that perhaps he wasn't coming.

Perhaps she'd be cooking a meal for two for one, especially considering the late hour now.

In her room on the second floor of the old Zick farmhouse, Molly knew she could learn whether her landlady was awake or not by peering down the bathroom vent, which let out into Mrs. Zick's bedroom. Normally, the old woman turned the light off by nine, and that was when Molly could be reasonably assured she'd gone to bed.

Just as the timer alerted her to check the pastries, a light flashed across the window in Molly's bedroom. She saw from her little kitchen, a flood of headlights that would otherwise never appear on a Sunday evening, even just off of Main Street.

Molly quickly checked the Palmiers, but by the time she'd made her way back to her bedroom window, whatever headlights had washed over Mrs. Zick's two-story home, had disappeared back into the cold, dark night.

So much for a romantic last-minute dinner with Liam Granger.

Molly prepared for the inevitability that she'd be storing half her meal for the woman who lived downstairs.

Chapter 33 — Liam

L iam studied the front door then looked back to the second floor bedroom where a light glowed low.

Maybe he should go home and get his phone charged up. But by then, the rush would well be gone.

He'd waited a week to talk to Molly. He'd waited months to feel normal after his dad's death. And before even that, he'd waited his whole life to feel *this* way about a girl.

Liam was done waiting.

Rubbing his hands together to fight the cold, he mounted the short stoop and stepped up to the front door. It was just the one. The last he'd been to Mrs. Zick's, he hadn't realized she was renting rooms, had he? Or maybe he had and he'd noticed then that this was no modern rental situation. This was more like an old-fashioned rooms for let situation, with a house mother—that'd be Mrs. Zick herself. Instead of name plates indicating who tenants were, there was just the house number.

Liam hesitated a moment, then pressed the doorbell.

Loud chimes—too loud—clanged from within, and he instantly realized his mistake.

A light flipped on in a nearby window, and the sounds of stumbling came next.

A couple of moments later, Mrs. Zick appeared in the slit of the door, her nose poking through and her lips asking, "Who's there?"

"Mrs. Zick, I'm so sorry—it's um, Liam Granger?"

"Liam what?" she croaked.

He wanted to die and took a step away from the door, trying to peer up at that second floor window and will Molly down from her chamber. "It's me, Mrs. Zick. Liam Granger. Larry Granger's son?"

The door closed, and the jangle of various locks clattered before she opened the door and popped her head out all the way this time, her eyes narrowing harshly. "Liam."

Before he could present the jar of raspberry jam, another voice came from behind Mrs. Zick.

"You're here!"

"Who is?" The old woman turned, and the front door fell open, and there, in the dimly lit foyer of the old Zick farmhouse stood an adorable looking Molly Maison, clad in plaid pajamas with a lace-trimmed apron tied over them. Her hair was a messy bun of cuteness piled up on her head, and, to Liam's further surprise, she wore glasses. Not for the first time, Liam wanted to scoop her up in his arms and haul her off to some private nook. He couldn't help it. Molly dragged out such feelings in him.

Molly expertly helped Mrs. Zick back into the house before waving Liam in. She then turned to a side table and picked up a covered plate. "Mrs. Zick, we're sorry to wake you."

"I wasn't asleep!" the old woman protested.

"I was up late cooking and invited Liam over to sample, but I figured you might like a plate too." She passed the plate to Mrs. Zick whose eyes lit up.

What came out of Liam's mouth next was the worst possible thing, but he was raised by a gentleman and a fretful aunt, and Liam couldn't help himself. "Mrs. Zick, would you like to join us? If it's all right by you, Molly?"

Behind Molly's eyes danced something, maybe, hopefully, the same exact dread that Liam was feeling over extending the invitation.

Thankfully, Mrs. Zick replied, "I wasn't asleep, but I *was* in bed. Anyhow, I'll have that for breakfast. Thank you!" She snatched away the plate and shooed Liam and Molly.

Suppressing their giggles, the pair made their way to the narrow wooden staircase which led darkly upstairs.

Once safely in Molly's room, Liam burst out with a sigh of relief. "I'm sorry. Maybe you didn't even invite me, but I had to come. And I had even brought this for Mrs. Zick, but—"

Molly took the jar of jam and set it on a small table by the door then stepped into Liam's arms and pressed herself against him.

He hugged her, and when they pulled apart, Molly looked up at Liam from behind her glasses, her mouth pouting and lips parted, and there was just one thing to be done.

So, Liam lowered his face to Molly's and kissed her as

gently as ever, savoring the softness of her lips and the smell of spices, sugars and shampoo. "You smell good," he whispered when they parted.

She grinned. "Come here."

He followed her into a small, makeshift kitchen where there was a miniature woodstove, a narrow, short fridge, and a counter. A delectable spread awaited him, and not for the first time it occurred to Liam that this was something often missing in his life—a good, homecooked meal.

He picked up one of the little cookies from the cooling rack. "What are these?"

"Palmiers. Elephant ears, some people call them."

"They look like little hearts," he remarked.

Molly slapped his hand, and he set the cookie down, startled. "No dessert until you've had your supper."

"Yes, ma'am." Liam leveled his jaw but couldn't stave off the grin that crept up his face.

They ate at a small wooden table that was crammed in between the fridge and the headboard of Molly's bed. Liam tried to ignore the fact that he was inches away from the very spot where Molly slept, but focusing on her food helped. It was scrumptious. Seasoned to perfection and cooked just so, he wondered if she'd be willing to do their Thanksgiving dinner, maybe. But that was an imposition, and the last thing Liam wanted was to impose on Molly. Especially considering all that had already been imposed upon her lately.

They lazily worked through the main course and vegetable sides before Molly finally brought over the cookies.

"Palmiers," Liam repeated. "Pronounced palm-ee-ays?"

Molly laughed. "Something like that. My mimi would know. She was the cook in the family. Everything I know, I learned from her."

"Is she still around?"

Molly shook her head. "She passed years ago. She was my father's mother, but actually my parents split up when I was little."

Liam nodded soberly. "I lost my mom too. Right after I was born. Or around that time, anyway."

Molly's face fell open in horror. Her hand moved to her mouth. "Oh, Liam. I'm so sorry."

He shrugged. "It's okay. I didn't know her, so I didn't have a chance to get my heart broken."

She eyed him, and that was all it took for him to break apart right then and there. Though he didn't cry, Liam felt emotionally split open. "I mean, not having had a mom around was pretty heartbreaking, I guess you could say. We made the best of it, though. My dad was really committed to raising me as a man's man."

"Ah." Molly smirked.

"What's that supposed to mean?"

"Nothing!" She threw her hands up, begging innocence. "White wine goes well with these because they are more buttery than sweet. You want a glass?"

"Sure."

"So," she said, as she poked into a narrow cupboard door and withdrew an unopened bottle, masterfully uncorking it and pouring two shallow glasses. She passed him one. "Your dad raised you alone. Never remarried? Or dated?"

"We had Betsy, and she was enough."

"Your aunt. Of course. Did she ever marry?"

"No. Betsy was too worried about me to date."

"That was probably hard on everyone. I don't mean to pry, but...did your mom just *leave*?"

Normally, Liam felt uneasy whenever anyone dug into his personal life like this. But with Molly, it felt different. "Um, that's a matter of who you ask."

Most people looked away, laughed uncomfortably, or brushed it all off. Molly held his gaze. "I'm asking you."

Liam's skin prickled with heat. "Actually, I don't know the full story. My dad says she left before I was even out of the hospital."

"What?" Molly's face twisted in shock.

"I know. It's...dramatic. My aunt is a little more weird about it. She says it's all a misunderstanding."

"What's there to misunderstand? Your mom left you after she'd just given birth? Can women even legally *do* that?"

"Yeah. I've wondered that too." Liam swallowed. "I guess I'll never know for sure."

"Did you ever try to contact her?"

"Did you ever try to contact your dad?" Liam shot back. He didn't mean to be short, but this conversation was going way deeper than what he'd expected.

Molly was unfazed. She pushed her glasses up the bridge of her nose and took a sip of her wine. "He made it clear he didn't want a family anymore."

"Well, so did my mom when she left." Liam shifted in his chair, then looked past Molly and around her little apartment. "This place is great."

"It's tiny, but I like it."

"You could use a bigger kitchen, probably."

"Yeah. That's true." She smiled back at Liam warmly. "Sorry about your mom. I shouldn't have pressed."

"Nah. I get it. A lot of people wonder why I never tried to find her. Sometimes I wonder that too. Sometimes I think maybe I'll start looking."

Molly said, "This is unrelated, but can I ask you something else?"

"Shoot."

"Have you ever, like, had a serious relationship?"

The tension that had crept up his spine vanished. He was back in his comfort zone, and this question was especially easy. "Nope. How about you?"

She shook her head. "Dating's not fun."

"I agree."

"Especially up here in these little South Dakota towns. You're stuck with the boys you grew up with or, like, your cousin twice removed."

"Yeah. I can relate."

"You're from here?" Molly seemed to be shifting inches closer as their back and forth sallied forth. Liam met her movement and scooted his wooden chair up an inch. He took a sip of his drink. Then a quick second.

"Um, no. Actually, I'm from Montana. Billings. That's where I graduated from high school. When we came here, my dad got the land from his dad, and the ranch and cabin was already here. We just had to make the rest work."

"You never went to college?"

Liam licked his lips. "Never wanted to." A frown coursed over his forehead. "Is that...a turnoff?"

149

Her eyes scrunched up. "A turnoff?" Then, she rolled them. "Hardly."

"Whew. You went to college. You're a teacher."

"Correct."

"Maybe you want a man with a degree." Their distance was closing in. She took a long last pull of her wine, and Liam mirrored the action, swallowing his and running the back of his hand over his mouth. Their knees brushed.

"You think I'm looking for a man?"

"You said you were dating. It was hard? Has it...gotten any easier since you've been in Prairie Creek?"

She sucked her lips into her teeth, and a bloom of color sprayed over her cheeks. "Ironically, it has."

"Why is that ironic?"

"Because Prairie Creek is, like, a quarter of the size of Aberdeen. Maybe even smaller. What about you?"

"What about me?" he asked, his chin lifted and looked down at her as if he was daring Molly.

She was unafraid. "Are you *looking*?"

Liam replied, "Not anymore."

Chapter 34—Molly

Molly arrived back at the ranch Monday after school. She had a fresh lease on things. Her mom was coming for Thanksgiving, and they'd be joining Liam and Betsy, and now Liam and Molly were...well, they had an understanding.

All Molly had to do was make it through to the festival, where she had grand plans.

Once Liam had left the night before—after sweet nothings over second glasses of wine, they had shared another sweet kiss, and then Liam, ever the gentleman, left.

Molly hadn't slept well, but when she woke in the morning, she felt inexplicably refreshed.

The kids were slated to handle various tasks that particular afternoon, and a lot of it had to do with livestock. With the hangar in good shape for the festival, this week would prove to be more ag training than Molly had yet to be subject to. And she was looking incredibly forward to it.

In fact, Molly was looking so forward to her second chance to train at the ranch, that she was beginning to wonder if she could perhaps take on teaching ag. Of course, only if the school would be willing to grant her culinary courses, too, but that was the big idea she'd come up with. Why couldn't she do it all? Wasn't that the adage of the modern woman? Wouldn't that satisfy everyone's needs? Molly thought yes.

Molly drove in tense silence with Penny, Dwayne, and Parker out to the ranch. The boys were on a tight leash with the rude comments, and Penny was also on her best behavior. So much so that she asked Molly, "Did Ms. Granger ever give you your clothes back, by the way?"

Molly told her no, not yet. It wasn't that she'd forgotten about the embarrassing outfit guffaw. She just hadn't had the chance to reach out over that. Anyway, she had other clothes. Currently, she wore a Mount Rushmore hoodie on top of a college hoodie on top of a thermal shirt over her backup jeans. It worked.

Once they arrived, Liam directed Penny to join Betsy in the kitchen to finish up some canning. Meanwhile the boys were off to chop wood.

This left Molly and Liam alone to talk about anything they wanted. Anything at all.

They could talk about applying the compost ahead of next week's storm. They could talk about how to look at the accounts and profitability of running a ranch—both more boring parts of Molly's training. They could even talk more about the festival, which by now was so well planned there wasn't much else to say.

There was something else Molly had needed to tell Liam, however. It was about Thanksgiving.

"So." She cleared her throat.

"Right, yeah," Liam jumped in. "I figure we can go check the ponds. Today was cold, and last night it got down below freezing."

"Check the ponds?"

"They're probably fine, but it's on that checklist of, um, the things we have to cover."

Checklist of things they had to cover? Checking the ponds? Her twisted expression gave way to further explanation when Liam went on. "Yeah, if creeks and ponds freeze up, cows can't drink. Soon enough, we'll provide troughs, but even so, it's important to keep the natural water sources accessible. Preparing the animals for the cold is critical. They need to go in well-nourished and healthy if they have hopes to survive a South Dakota winter."

"Right." Molly followed him to the big shed where he pulled some tools down. Once they took off across the pasture, she worked up her courage again. "By the way, Liam. About, um, Thanksgiving."

Liam looked at her. "Thanksgiving, yeah." A smile twitched over his mouth, but he hid it with a serious drop of his eyebrows. "Well, I can answer anything. Mainly, we do the usual—turkey, stuffing, dressing, sides. Desserts. It's a lot of work when you combine it with the festival the next day and the community dinner right after that, but my dad and Betsy always insisted on having just a Granger family affair." He stopped.

Molly stopped, too, looking around and wondering if they'd come across the first pond.

She didn't see water but in the distance, the boys were baling alfalfa together. One driving the tractor and the other spotting, as it appeared.

Molly turned around to see if she could also spy Penny, but she couldn't. Betsy was out of sight too. If she and Liam continued walking forward, they'd meet up with Parker and Dwayne.

"Let's go this way." Liam said almost as though he could read her mind. They cut east along a thatch of brambles that carried off into the distance. The sun would set at their back if they were out long. More than that, they'd get mighty cold out there on the prairie. Molly was worried her layers weren't enough. Even two sweatshirts didn't compare to the Carhartt.

The conversation was stilted in a tantalizing way. It was less a conversation than it was a chess match, and now it was again Molly's move.

"It sounds great. Your Thanksgiving dinner, I mean."

"Thanks. It'll be different this year, but..." his voice drifted off into the cold afternoon air.

Molly wanted to melt into the grass right then. *Of course.* She squeezed her eyes shut then opened them again and said, "I'm really sorry. I imagine the holidays are going to be hard."

Liam was quiet a moment. "Every day gets easier, but I'd be lying if I said there wasn't part of my heart that was dreading Thursday. And Friday. And all of December pretty much." A short laugh spilled out, but when Molly looked up at him, his face was free of any smile.

"Um, speaking of the dinner." She didn't want to change the topic but she didn't know how to talk to someone so steeped in grief. "Not sure if I mentioned this. Um. My mom is actually supposed to come to town?" Why she said it like a question, Molly couldn't say.

"Oh, of course. I meant to tell you that your family is welcome too. Especially your mom."

"I think she's going to help me with the festival."

"That's great." He was being genuine, but guilt bubbled up in Molly. Not guilt, exactly, but *something*. The need to confess how much the festival meant for her, maybe?

It was Molly's turn to stop. She sighed. "I have to win Mr. Porter over. And the board."

"Win them over?" He laughed and pushed his fingers through his hair. She could kiss him for how easy he seemed to approach life. Like nothing was win or lose, life or death, even though he had very recently experienced just that thing. Maybe it was the male perspective or maybe it was that Molly's career fears were so deep that she saw the contrast between her insecurities and in other people's confidence.

"I don't mind this." She indicated the ranch. "And obviously I *love* working alongside you, which is insane."

He pulled her into his side, but Molly glanced around to be sure even their briefest affections went unnoticed. "I love your being here too."

She winced. "But I want to teach Culinary Arts. My dream is to carry on my mimi's legacy. French cooking in the heart of America. It's who I am. Where I come from. I can't just give it up, even if it's extremely tempting. Which, it is." Shamelessly, she batted her eyelashes up at Liam who bit his lower lip hard. The silent gesture proved they were very much on the same wavelength. It was painful to be so close and have to act so far away from one another.

155

"I get that, though." They continued walking. Liam went on, "Sometimes, I wonder what I was destined for."

"It's not ranching?"

He was quiet a moment. "Honestly, ranching is close, it's just—a lot. And that would be fine if I weren't kind of alone."

Molly's heart pounded at the implication, even though really, it meant nothing. But that was the thing about implications. They could mean everything. She said, "You have Betsy."

He threw his head back and pushed a sigh out. "When my dad was around, we hired out a lot of the help, and that worked. But then, what's really the point? Money? Fine. The ranch is self-sustaining now that I unloaded a lot of our animals. I could sell some of the acreage off and invest it and be fine." He slid his gaze her way. "That sounds braggy."

"I could brag, too, you know."

"Oh yeah?" His grin widened.

"Oh yeah. I rent this fabulous room in the heart of Prairie Creek, and did you know a celebrity lives there? Oh yeah, and I can cook a mean Palmier. Did I mention my chicken?"

"Or your peanut butter sammies, for that matter." He winked at her.

"And you haven't even *tried* my Thanksgiving roast and fixings."

"Will I get to?"

"I'll cook, sure. It's what I do, after all."

"I can help."

"I'll need all the help I can get." Molly thought for a

moment. Now felt like a good time to divulge a little of her past. "Did I tell you my mimi owned a café in France?"

"No, but that's extremely cool. Is that what you want? To run a restaurant or something?"

Molly beamed. "Nope. I just want to teach, like my mom. I love working with kids—I love kids. The cooking is the end goal, but the process is all about sharing...sharing my love with the next generation? Is that super cheesy?"

"Only if it's a cheesy dish. Can you do a great melt?"

"The best."

"That'd be pretty cheesy, then."

She rolled her eyes. "Mimi was my dad's mom, actually. And we lived with her when my dad left." Molly wasn't sure why she was saying this. Maybe it had to do with walking through the chilly prairie with Liam, huddled deep in her jacket but not wholly removed from the sparks of electricity that buzzed in the air between them.

Liam stopped again, and when Molly looked down, she saw they stood at a brook. Babbling water coursed in a narrow stream from north to south, splicing the ranch. "It's not frozen."

Molly agreed with a nod.

Liam said, "You learned to cook from your mimi and you lived with her. You were really close, huh?"

"Yes. Very close. All growing up, I looked forward to going home to Mimi so I could see what we were making for supper." Even now, Molly pictured a smaller version of herself, shedding her coat and backpack by the door, slipping out of her galoshes and into an apron and washing up only to quickly find herself covered from head to toe in flour, egg batter, sugar, and spices. The smell of cloves was permanently stamped in her brain anytime the image of Mimi came to mind.

Liam turned to face Molly. In the distance beyond him, the cabin and Betsy's cottage, the outbuildings and machines were splashes of color on a browning landscape. It might have been in this very moment that the seasons changed for Molly. When she looked out across the wide-open plains, autumn had consumed the world. Trees were naked of their leaves, save for the evergreens. The grasses that grew on the edges of the pasture had long lost their color, even though the clovers at Molly's feet glowed the color of Christmas trees.

Molly met Liam's stare. "What?" she asked, wrapping her arms around herself subconsciously.

Liam ran his hand up the back of his head. He looked back towards the rest of his property then out into the great beyond of the South Dakota countryside. Then he looked again at Molly. "You know exactly what you want, but here you are, doing something else entirely." He said this with some measure of awe.

Liam took a step closer to her.

Her breath caught in her chest. She nodded, but her head felt like it was bobbing on the brook at her heels, floating, spinning, and drifting dizzyingly away from her body.

"That's why..." her voice drifted away. She hadn't mentioned to anyone but her mom about the job application. She hadn't even come to terms with the decision herself. And yet, she knew she *had* to create opportunities for herself. If she didn't, she might always regret not following her dream.

Molly looked down and sputtered a short laugh.

"Maybe we aren't all cut out to follow our dreams. Maybe I'm being unrealistic."

"You don't believe that."

She looked up, sharp. "What?"

"If you believed that, you wouldn't be here."

"You're wrong."

"I'm right. You talk like you've given up, but you don't pay attention to half the things I say. If you had given up on your dream and given into ag, you'd have been listening to me this whole time." He gave her a wry smile.

"As a matter of fact, I do too listen." She fell back half a step and pushed her hands out her sleeves and hooked them in the crooks of her arms, giving him a harder stare. "I pay attention."

"Okay, when is calving season?"

"We didn't cover that."

"What is silage?"

"Silage is...it's like *silo*, I think."

"Why do we draw the herd to different pastures throughout the winter?"

"To give them exercise?"

Liam laughed. "You haven't learned a thing, but I know you're smart. Every minute you spend here, your mind is a thousand miles away."

"And how do you know that?"

"Your eyes."

"My *eyes*." Molly rolled them. "You don't know anything about me."

"I know what Parker and Penny Porter say. And Dwayne too. And Phil. I know what Betsy says and the school board. I know more than you think."

"You know what the school board says?" Molly felt her heart freeze over. "So this was all *your* idea."

"What was all my idea?" he shot back.

"This!" Molly spread her arms out. "You needed help! You lied and pretended you didn't. You wanted to look like a real man or something, but you *needed* me."

"Why would I *need* you?" He raised his voice to match hers.

"Because!" She was all but shouting now.

"Because *why*? I was ready to close this whole place down. Sold off half the livestock. I didn't need help. I still don't."

"Then what are they?" Molly pointed toward the tractor rumbling across the pasture. "And Penny? And what am *I* doing here? You just said yourself that ranching is too hard, because you need more help."

His jaw set and nostrils flared. She saw he'd dropped his pond tapping tools to the bed of grass beneath their feet. "I can hire out help. I never needed a schoolteacher to come here for me to train her, you know."

"But you needed the kids to hire, and they were falling in love with a different class. Culinary Arts." Her voice was soft, but her words were meant to prick him like pins.

"You know what, Molly? You're right. I said I needed help if I was going to keep the ranch going. But I wasn't." He shrugged listlessly.

Liam stared at her, and from his cool eyes, she didn't see anger but sadness. "Liam, I'm sorry. I never should have accused you, it's just that I don't feel like I know my place in the world anymore. My goal was to have this amazing career, and now here I am."

"Testing ponds for freeze," Liam finished her thought. He reached for Molly's hands and she let him take them. "We can fix that, you know."

"*We*?" She raised a skeptical eyebrow.

"It was my aunt's fault. She thought you were amazing the first time she met you."

"What do you mean?"

He sighed out long and heavily. "Betsy pitched to the board the idea of bringing back ag with you at the helm. I know. I *know*. It was a terrible thing for her to have done."

"She didn't want Culinary Arts at the school?"

"No, no, *no*. That wasn't it at all." He scrunched up his face. "She wanted there to be a reason for you and me to spend time together, I guess. A poor attempt at match-making maybe?"

"Like, you and me?" Molly's heart lifted at that, ridiculously.

"Yeah. I know. And I'm *sorry*. She didn't mean for you to become some permanent replacement. She thought maybe the district could have their cake and eat it too. And she thought you and I would hit it off."

"Did we?" Molly's voice dipped low, and she stepped closer to Liam, impervious to the idea that they might be found out again. Maybe she even *wanted* to be found out. Maybe it could fix things for her.

Liam must also have given up on caring about some guise of professionalism. He slid his hands from hers then wrapped them around her waist and pressed his forehead into Molly's. "Obviously," he whispered.

Molly moved her face away for the moment it took to reposition her mouth, and as though Liam could read her mind, he kissed her. Harder than before, their lips opening and working in a delirious rhythm.

Finally, when they pulled back, hearts pounding, pulses racing and lips swollen, concern struck Liam's features. "What is it, Molly?"

She was falling for Liam, but her heart wasn't one hundred percent there on the Granger Ranch, and it was time she spoke up.

"What if they don't bring back Culinary Arts?"

Without her having to explain, he knew. He understood very clearly that Molly could not go on teaching agriculture. And even if it was a useful thing for her to have learned about, and even if she was happy to pitch in and be Liam's ranch hand girlfriend or whatever this was...still, she needed her classroom. Her kitchen. Her students with flour caked into their chubby teenage knuckles and sugar sticky on the bottoms of their shoes.

Liam replied simply. Confidently. "They will."

Chapter 35 — Liam

He was in over his head with that promise, but Liam would drown for Molly.

And while, yes, he had some power with the school board, his aunt was on it. And yes, he had some sway with Phil Porter—his dad's best friend. But there wasn't much a single person could do about a small town who'd become unquenchably thirsty for a single goal.

That's when, Tuesday morning, it occurred to him. There absolutely *was* something he could do. It might work. It might not, but it was the one idea within Liam's power to help Molly reclaim her culinary program.

First, he would have to get his aunt's blessing. Nothing happened at the ranch without the explicit approval of the matriarch of Granger Ranch.

Chapter 36 — Molly

Molly woke up Tuesday feeling a little less conflicted than she had on Monday. Liam was fast becoming a staple in her every thought, and she knew he now owned a part of her heart. That much was clear.

And maybe there was a chance she could just do ag as her teaching job. Nobody said Molly couldn't start an after school cooking club. Maybe that'd satisfy her longing to fulfill the Maison legacy. Or what if she *did* open a restaurant in town? She could name it Mimi's, after Mimi, of course. The possibilities really were endless.

Which was why, when she got a phone call during lunch, everything became even harder.

The number was unfamiliar, but the area code indicated Aberdeen. Worried it might be her mom calling from school or maybe a colleague to deliver some terrible news, Molly answered immediately. "Hello?"

"Hi, I'm calling for Molly Maison."

"This is Molly."

"Hello, Molly. My name is Rita Vertrees. I'm the principal at—"

Molly completed the woman's sentence on instant. "The high school. In Aberdeen." In her mind, she added, *the one I applied to*.

"That's right!"

Molly's mind swirled with what might come next. Hopefully, it wouldn't be an offer that she couldn't refuse.

"Molly, I know your mother, Jean. She's so wonderful, by the way."

Maybe Molly was wrong. "Thank you."

"But that's not why I'm calling."

"Oh?"

"No. Molly, we'd love to schedule an interview with you for the Culinary Arts teaching position. Are you available tomorrow, by chance? I know you're out of town. We'd be happy to conduct the interview on the phone or by video."

Molly's mouth fell open. She stared blankly at her lunch, a Croque Monsieur she'd whipped up in her little office. A hot ham and cheese sandwich, this included béchamel sauce, ham, cheese, and a dash of Dijon mustard. Grilled up on a hot plate she kept for quick projects. "Interview?"

Should Molly say no? Should she say that, yes, she desperately wanted to teach Culinary Arts, but unfortunately she was also falling in love and the pressure to choose between these two dreams was too much to handle and she was going to *burst*—

Her classroom door cracked open, and through it, Penny Porter's head appeared. "Miss Maison?"

Molly didn't have the bandwidth to juggle both the

woman on the phone *and* the girl at her door. Instinctively, she responded to Penny. "Yes."

The woman on the phone replied in Molly's ear. "Wonderful!"

But before Molly could say *no, I was talking to someone else,* it was too late. The wheels were in motion. Penny was bounding into the classroom chattering about the pie recipe she had for Friday's festival, and Rita Vertrees was putting together a time for a phone call. First thing in the morning.

The future was no longer in Molly's hands.

Chapter 37 — Liam

Molly and her trio of misfits arrived Tuesday afternoon, but Liam detected a change. He hadn't made enough headway on his big plans yet to reveal them to Molly, but by the time they were alone together in the hangar, dressing up each of the tables in greenery and tinsel, he knew it was important he say *something*.

After all, she seemed like she needed hope. She seemed quiet.

"So, I've been thinking," he said.

Molly looked up from where she was securing brown paper along her own festival table.

"Is that new for you?" She gave him a playful look, and it was everything he needed. The back-and-forth. The flirtation. He relaxed immediately.

"Ha. Ha."

She finished the paper and smoothed her hands over the top of it, and images flashed through Liam's mind. In three days' time, the hangar would be filled with Creek folk,

Christmas music, and holiday bustle. And in *two* days' time, he'd be meeting Molly's mom. The pressure was suffocating him.

"Well, I was just thinking about you and the culinary thing and—"

"And how you're going to fix everything for me?" She gave him a pitiful look. "Liam, I've been thinking too, actually." Her brows stitched together, and it made his heart drop.

"Thinking?"

"This whole mess isn't yours. I mean, maybe Betsy had something to do with it, yeah. But her good intentions were just that. Good intentions. If it's meant to be that I'm not going to teach Culinary Arts in Prairie Creek, then it's meant to be."

He balked. "What's that supposed to mean?"

"What I mean is, maybe I stay here and do ag. I help you on the ranch. Then, in the evenings, I teach a teen cooking class. There are so many options. Really."

His heart rebounded, but he still knew that Molly's idea didn't solve the problem. She deserved to have her dreams. And it was his obligation, as the man who was falling fast for her, to make sure she came to realize them. "Molly, I have to get something off my chest." The words were flowing from his heart to his lips and soon enough he'd rounded the table and come up to Molly, reaching for her hands.

"Okay?" She looked nervous.

"No, it's—nothing big. Just that, listen, Molly. I really like you. Like, *a lot*. And I want you to have everything in the world. Everything you want, but selfishly, I want that thing to be me. *Here*."

She blinked at him and chewed her lower lip adorably. "I like you, too, Liam. Like, *a lot*."

He could have melted. "But Prairie Creek doesn't have what you need."

Molly's smile slipped.

"No, don't—no, that's not. I'm saying this all wrong. Listen, Molly, I'm going to do everything in my power to get your program back. But if I can't..."

"If you can't, then I will still be falling for you."

He beamed. "If I can't, I want you to follow your dreams. I don't want to be some force blocking that."

She frowned and pulled her hands from his. "I don't understand."

"Molly, I'm going to do everything in my power to convince the school to give you Culinary Arts. To keep Culinary Arts. To kick ag to the corner, if they have to."

"And if you fail, you think I should just, what? Leave?"

"No." He'd screwed up. He was saying everything wrong, and Molly couldn't read minds or hearts, and she didn't know that what was on his was a mix of love, or the beginnings of it, and of fear. Ultimately, Liam knew that the future would be grim for a couple in which one of them had to give up a dream for the other one. Liam didn't have a dream, and so it'd be hardly fair for Molly to give everything for him. To sacrifice it all, for *him*.

But Molly had stopped listening and had started backing up. "I appreciate it, really, Liam."

"Molly, no. Wait. That's not what I meant. I don't want you to leave. Please." But he couldn't very well just say he

169

was going to sell the ranch and force the school board's hand toward the culinary program because that was a promise he couldn't make. And Liam, better than anyone, understood what happened when you made a promise you couldn't keep. It broke people's hearts. The last thing he wanted to do was break Molly's heart.

But here he was, doing exactly that.

Chapter 38 — Molly

E verything was ready enough for Thanksgiving and for the festival. Pies were assigned to students. Ingredients secured. The turkey was thawing nicely in Liam's cabin, and Molly's mom was excited to meet the people who lived in her daughter's new little world.

And still, Molly was petrified. Petrified that Liam didn't actually want her to stay. Petrified that he wasn't falling as hard for her as she was for him. Petrified that staying in Prairie Creek would result in dashed dreams and nothing more.

So when she took the interview phone call with Rita Vertrees, Molly went all in. It was the only thing she knew to do. She talked recipes and classroom management, her resourcefulness and cooperative attitude. She laid everything out there.

And when the interview was over, Rita said point blank, "Molly, you're exactly what we're looking for."

The words crippled Molly. "I am?" she asked half-heartedly.

"You are, yes. Listen, we want to offer you a teaching contract. Here, you would have a fully furnished and stocked kitchen. Access to vocational education funds. Pathway programs for your students to move from your classroom to a post-secondary culinary school. Quarterly performance-based bonuses. Oh, and this is a full-time teaching position with benefits. In fact, we would *love* for you to start in January, if that's a possibility. If not, next school year is great. We are desperate for a fabulous Culinary Arts teacher. And, Molly, that's clearly *you*."

Chapter 39 — Liam

Wednesday evening, after Molly and the kids and Betsy had all called it a day, Liam held Molly back from the bus. "Can I talk to you?"

She glanced after her students. "Sure. Actually, I meant to ask you—can I get my clothes back?"

This single, innocent question gutted him. Molly thought Liam didn't want her around, and this was the furthest thing from the truth. Wasn't it?

"Um. Yeah. Tomorrow, maybe?"

"That's fine."

"You're still coming, aren't you? Bringing your mom too?"

Molly smiled thinly. "Of course. You have my turkey, after all."

He tried for a heartfelt grin, but knew that they were on brittle ice, much like the ice that had begun to creep over the ponds across his ranch. "I just wanted to see if we're okay?"

"We?" Her face opened, but a shadow quickly crossed it. "Yes. The kids are ready for Friday. I'm ready. We'll eat together tomorrow. Everything is *fine*."

"I'm still working on your culinary program." The words came out shallow and lifeless, and Liam felt sick about that, but ultimately, all he had done so far was to talk to Betsy. She'd been hesitant to support him, reminding him that his idea would cripple their livelihood and change everything. Her reluctance had him second guessing.

"Okay." He flicked a glance up to the bus, willing the watchful eyes of the three kids away so he could give her a quick peck on the cheek. Molly reached down and gave his hand a quick squeeze, as though she knew what he wanted to do, and she wanted it too. It was enough to keep him going. To keep him hoping.

To keep him digging into his own heart to find an answer.

It took every ounce of strength in his soul to get to the bottom of how he was feeling, which was why Liam decided to spend the rest of the evening with Georgie, in his bedroom.

At his dad's chest.

Sure enough, every answer Liam had ever needed had been right there, at his feet, beneath the snoozing body of his best friend, all along.

Chapter 40 — Liam

Liam asked Betsy to come early the next morning. There was something he had to tell her.

She arrived makeup-less, in casual clothes, with her favorite coffee mug in hand. "I think I know what this is about," she said as she held out the mug for him to fill it up.

"You do?"

"You finally went through the chest."

Liam stared at his aunt, anger coursing through his veins. "You *knew*."

"I'm sorry, hon." Her eyes pleaded with Liam. "Your dad was convinced that knowing the truth would be harder than believing a lie. Your dad was scared, I think. He was scared that you'd blame yourself."

If that was true, then Liam could cobble together some understanding. His dad would have been right. Liam would have blamed himself. He'd never have dated or married or had children for fear that the love of his life might die.

Instead, he had never dated or married or had children for fear that the love of his life would leave him.

And here he was, telling her to do just that.

"What was in the chest?" Betsy asked.

He frowned. "You said you knew."

"I knew the truth. I don't know what was in there that would eventually reveal it to you."

Liam swallowed. His heart had been shattered the night before to learn the truth about his mom. The truth that she didn't just leave them. That his dad's warnings against the flighty hearts of women was a deception. That his dad had taken his own heartbreak and ensured it would live on in Liam. For all the wrong reasons.

"My mother's death certificate," he said, his voice breaking as he verbalized the fact that not only had he been grieving his father's death, but now, too, would he begin to grieve his mother's. The mother who did not leave Liam. Not intentionally. The mother who loved her husband and her son. Who never would have left them. Never would have broken their hearts.

The mother who died in childbirth.

"Oh, honey." Betsy pulled Liam into a tight hug, patting his back and shushing him like a mother would. "My sweet Liam, it's okay. Shh. Shhh."

Through choking sobs, he managed, "Why didn't he tell me the *truth*? It might have changed things."

Betsy pulled herself from him and squeezed his shoulders. "Liam, even if you had the truth and lived according to that, what would it have changed?"

"Everything," he whispered.

But his aunt was unmoved. "No." Sternly, she shook a

finger at him. "You have two choices, Liam Lawrence Granger. You can let this unearthed secret ruin you. Or you can let it save you."

"Save me?"

"What have you just learned? You've learned that what you thought all these years—that love was fleeting—you learned you were wrong."

"My dad misled me."

"You took one thing and let it grow into your lens. You took your mother's absence, God rest her soul, and applied it to every opportunity you ever had. You let it color your world dark and grim. You let it stunt you. And now, you have the truth. What are you going to do with that, Liam?"

Liam held his aunt's gaze. The answer was simple. "I know exactly what I'm going to do."

Chapter 41—Molly

Rita Vertrees told Molly she could have the long weekend to make her decision. By Monday, Molly would call her back and tell her that no, she wasn't accepting the offer. Or, yes, she was accepting her dream job.

Spending Thanksgiving Day at Liam's did not help matters.

Molly's mom drove down to Prairie Creek and stopped first at Mrs. Zick's, where the pair were about to pile into Molly's car when the old lady hobbled out of her room and inquired about where Molly was off to. Molly couldn't believe that she hadn't considered this before, but did Mrs. Zick have anywhere to spend Thanksgiving? She'd hate to show up with an unexpected plus-one to the ranch, but she couldn't just leave the poor old woman there alone.

Jean looked at Molly then back at Mrs. Zick. "We're going out to this homestead where Molly works," she replied on her daughter's behalf.

Molly shrank inside. She thought through what Liam

would think and what Miss Betsy would think, and then she remembered that tomorrow, after the festival, Liam hosted the community supper. Maybe Mrs. Zick would just go to that?

Still, it wasn't enough.

Mrs. Zick, dressed to the nines in a rhinestone-trimmed, burgundy cotton set, with a knit scarf hanging out of one hand said, "A homestead? You know this right here used to be a homestead. A farm, we called it. When my husband passed, we sold off so much of it. It's nothing like it used to be. A homestead. How quaint."

"Remember, Mrs. Zick?" Molly asked. "The Granger Ranch. Liam Granger."

"Oh, yes. The young man who brought me goods. He was just here the other night."

Jean gave Molly a knowing look, and Molly knew she had to throw suspicion off lest her mom beg for details that didn't yet exist. "You know what, Mrs. Zick? We'd love you to join us, if you don't have other holiday plans?"

"Oh, dear!" Mrs. Zick's eyes lit up. "I'd love to go with you to your little homestead holiday."

Chapter 42 — Liam

Nerves took over as soon as Georgie yipped the announcement that guests had arrived.

His plan was in place, and Betsy was in the loop. The turkey was roasting, per Molly's instructions. Sides were underway.

The table was set.

But when Liam went to answer the door, he found that Molly had brought more than just her mother.

"Mrs. Zick?" He was confused, at first, by the old woman's presence.

Molly was quick to explain. "I hope it's okay. I invited Mrs. Zick along for dinner. She was all dressed up with nowhere to go."

Liam's heart melted even more over Molly, if that was possible. "Of course." He gave the old woman a quick peck on the cheek and escorted her in. Then, he turned his attention to Molly and the other woman with her. "You must be Mrs. Maison."

"Jean." The woman was tall and dark haired, like Molly.

Lean and beautiful. Liam would be remiss not to point out that Molly took after her mother. "It's so nice to meet the person who brought Molly into the world." He fumbled over the words and cringed at his own awkwardness, but behind Jean, Molly was giggling. Her smile and laughter gave him all the courage he needed to move through the dinner and get to the point where he had his big announcement.

Dinner went well. Betsy said grace, and the turkey and fixings were all divine. Mrs. Zick reminisced about her youth. Jean told everyone silly stories about when Molly was little.

Betsy regaled the group with the tale of the day they moved onto the ranch, and how Liam didn't know a hammer from a saw.

"I was a quick learner," he added.

"So, Molly, tell us, how do you like working at Prairie Creek High?" Betsy asked Molly after plates were cleared and pumpkin pie was dished out.

Liam braced for impact. This was his opening. Betsy had lobbed a softball for him to swing away.

But Molly's response threw everything off track.

Chapter 43 — Molly

Molly had not made her decision. Not outwardly, anyway.

But the moment she sat down to supper with her mom, Liam, Betsy, and even old Mrs. Zick, something in her flipped. Utterly at home there, eating the turkey that Liam prepared—very well, she might add—and sipping on cranberry wine and laughing over stories from her childhood and Liam's, and even her landlady's, Molly realized she couldn't imagine leaving. Not now or in January. Not even next summer, before the start of a new school year.

When Betsy opened the conversation to Molly and her work, it felt like the right time to come out with her secret. "Actually," she said, dabbing her lips and stealing a glance at Liam, who sat directly across from her. "It's been a strange semester."

He cocked his head, and under the small wooden table that was crowded with the five of them, she felt something slide along the inside of her boot. She looked at him and he nodded. Was this a secret message? Was it a warning?

"Because of the ag program." Betsy clicked her tongue and shook her head and ripped Molly's attention from the sensation at the inside of her foot and to the woman who sat at the head of the table. "Molly, I am so sorry for all of that. It was my fault. I wanted you and Liam to become acquainted, and I brought up the idea of maybe plugging you into the hole and—" she looked down at her lap then back up at Molly. "I'm sorry, hon."

"It's fine. Really. I think the community wants agriculture to remain securely in the school system here."

Again, she could feel Liam's hot gaze on her. Warning her. Promising her. Tempting her to look back at him and say, *Spit it out.*

Instead, she broke with her news. "I applied for a job in Aberdeen."

An audible gasp escaped Betsy's mouth, which she quickly covered with a worried hand. Betsy's gaze flew about the table. "What? No!"

Molly looked at her mom, who nodded encouragingly, then she opened her mouth to continue, but Liam stopped her. "Molly, wait."

"What?"

"I'm giving up the ranch."

"What?" Molly was confused. "What do you mean?" And what did that have to do with *her* news?

He pushed his chair back and shot up out of it. "Can we—Molly. I need to talk to you."

"What's going on?" She looked around in bewilderment.

"Alone?" he asked. Then, more desperately, "*Please.*"

Jean and Betsy exchanged a knowing look right across the table, and Mrs. Zick, who was blissfully out of the loop, asked for a refill of wine.

Molly got up and followed Liam through the kitchen and living room, down the hall and into his bedroom.

She felt like she was seeing it for the first time. Her senses attune now, she took the space in anew.

It smelled like Liam, pine scented, fresh, and musky. His bed, a pinewood framed queen with neatly tucked flannel sheets and a heavy, cozy quilt pulled tight, stood in the center, against a picture window that looked out across the ranch.

In the center of the bed lay a dry cleaner's bag—or, that's what it looked like anyway. Paper, not plastic, and long, it draped over the foot of the bed, its bottom falling across a heavy wooden chest.

Molly blinked at it, then at Liam. "What is it?"

He moved to shut the door behind her, which made their escape to the room tenfold more intimate and also a little risky.

Molly liked that, but wondered what the others were thinking.

As if reading her mind, Liam said. "Don't worry about them. Betsy will catch your mom up to speed. I just wanted to tell you my plan. Before you tell me you're going to take that job in Aberdeen and follow your dream, I want to tell you that, Molly," his face pinched in pain and fear, "I wasn't joking when I said I was falling for you. I'm *really* falling for you, and although I would never ask you to give up your dream for me, who you hardly know, I'm ready to give up the world just for a chance to love you."

Molly had never known that a person's knees could physically, actually go weak. "Love?" The word floated out on a breath.

"Maybe we're not there yet, and who knows what happens down the road, but, um..." he scratched the back of his head and gave her a sheepish look. "Yeah. I think I could love you. I think I'm falling *in* love with you. Your beauty and your mind. Your heart. Your abilities. The whole thing, Molly. You're incredible."

She looked at him like he might be an alien. Like he'd known her actions even when she hadn't.

"What do you mean you're ready to give up your world? What does that mean?" she asked, fretfully.

"After this year, I'm closing the ranch. For good. Without a cooperating ranch, there can be no agriculture program at the school. Phil Porter will find he has no choice. He can bring Culinary Arts back, or he can face the wrath of families whose kids have fallen as in love with you as I have."

Chapter 44 — Liam

Molly's eyes closed for half a breath and when she opened them, she said, "You don't have to do that."

"I wanted to." But was he too late? Should he have made a grand gesture like this days earlier, before she'd had a chance to go out and apply to work in another town? "But if you want to go, I support that too. As long as I can visit you."

"You won't have to," Molly whispered.

"What?" He *was* too late. Liam pressed his mouth in a line. "You took the job, didn't you?"

Tears welled up in her eyes, but she laughed as she wiped them away. "No. I turned it down."

"What?"

"Yeah, I know. It was, like, my *dream* job. A full-time culinary position. Kitchen. Funding. The works."

"Are you crazy?" he was pulling her into him, kissing her cheeks, her tears, her smile. "Molly, you're *crazy*." He burrowed his face into her hair, and when he came up for air, he held her gaze for a long moment. "Why didn't you take it?"

"Why do you think?" She ran her hands up his chest and bit her lower lip.

"Not for me. Please, no."

"Oh, so...you're *not* selling the ranch?" Here they were again, toying with each other. At least, she was toying with him.

"I'm not selling it. Not the rest of it, no. I'm simply not cooperating with the school. No student training program. No courses. Not here. And, seeing as this is the last working ranch in twenty-five miles, that puts quite the burden on the district."

Molly marveled at him. "What did Mr. Porter say?"

"He is going to talk to you at the festival tomorrow. I think he has a proposal. Though I can't say if it'll be quite as good as the offer you got out of Aberdeen."

"I don't care about that offer."

"Of course you do, because you care about your career."

"I care about *you*, Liam. And about what could be if I stay right where I am."

"Here?"

Their hands laced up, and their voices dropped. Molly whispered, "Right here."

"Like *here* here?" he asked with a crooked grin. "On my homestead?"

"Well, some days, yeah. Other days, who knows where we'll be. Maybe in my second floor room at Mrs. Zick's?"

"Or at the school, in your classroom."

"Or milking cows or goats or checking ponds for freeze."

"You'll need your Carhartt for that, you know." He pulled away from her and turned to the bed, scooping up the hanger and its paper bag.

"Is that—" Molly pointed.

"I took it to the Thimble Shoppe on Main Street. Mabel knew just what to do." He untaped the paper to reveal Molly's jacket, completely refurbished. Almost like new. "She fixed it for you."

Molly took it, examined the seams, and studied it for a long beat. "Does this mean I still have to work at the ranch?"

"Homestead, remember?"

"Oh, right. Homestead."

"And all it means is that if you need me, I'll do whatever I can, Molly Maison. I'll eat your gourmet peanut butter sandwiches and deliver fresh milk and butter to you. I'll get your clothes sewn up and your classroom stove working. I'll muscle knuckleheads into taking Culinary Arts. I'll do whatever it takes to show you that Prairie Creek doesn't need an ag program. It needs Molly Maison. And so do I."

Molly hugged the jacket to her chest, and Liam wrapped her up in his arms, dipping his mouth to hers and kissing her long and good and completely free from the nosey eyes of students or others. It was their first kiss like this, secluded, and so much of him wanted to swing her up and over to his bed and kiss her longer and harder. But they had company in the kitchen, and two slices of pumpkin pie that hadn't been touched.

And a festival tomorrow.

And, with any luck, a whole lifetime ahead of them for haystack kisses and bedroom embraces.

Chapter 45 — Molly

After their kiss, Molly pulled away and looked up at Liam, her heart pounding with hope and happiness. "I have a couple of phone calls to make," she said. "To that principal in Aberdeen."

"But it's a holiday. Can't the principal wait?"

"She can. But I can't." Molly pushed up on her tiptoes and kissed Liam again, knowing she wanted to leave a message right now. She wanted to tell the world that she wasn't leaving Prairie Creek. That she was staying. That maybe she'd been offered her dream somewhere else, but actually, she'd already started to make her dream come true right there, in the little town which didn't know how much they needed Molly Maison and her culinary expertise.

Liam asked, "And who else do you need to call?"

"Mr. Porter."

Liam reminded her, "Just wait. He said he's going to find you at the festival. He'll have something to offer you, I promise."

"How do you know that? Is it because you forced his hand?" It was meant as a joke but the words stung.

Liam's features turned serious. He framed Molly's face in his hands and lifted it to him. "No. It's because you're good at what you do, and people can see that, Molly. People here believe in you."

She closed her eyes and tried to shake her head. A single tear poured from one eye and spilled over her cheek. In that moment, she thought about her mimi, her legacy. Her mother, her role model. And now Liam, who told her exactly what she needed to hear.

He wiped the tear from her cheek and pressed his mouth again to hers. Molly kissed him back, and when they parted once more, she asked him, "You know what I believe in?"

"What?" he whispered.

"*Us.*"

Chapter 46 — Molly

The festival was a hit, and Molly had never seen anything like it.

Having grown up in Aberdeen, she thought she knew what a small town function looked like, but she had no idea.

Every booth was decked out—hers and Liam's doing—and packed with goods for sale. She got to meet Logan Ryerson, Griffin Dempsey, and Mabel Ryerson, whom she thanked for a beautiful job on her jacket. She even got to meet the famous Kelly Watts, who did not compete with Molly by way of selling baked goods or any food at all. Instead, she was there simply to shop. When the celebrity herself sampled Penny's mulberry pie, she melted to the floor in a dramatic show. "This is *delectable*. I *must* get the recipe from you!" Penny had beamed, and Molly had just about died from shock at the entire experience. But when Kelly went so far as to ask for Molly's cell number so they *could get together and talk shop*, Molly was even more certain that she had made the right decision to stay.

Once Kelly had sashayed away in a pretty pioneer dress over stockings and boots—ultra fashionable, adorable, and cozy—Molly had waved Liam over.

"Kelly Watts wants one of *my* recipes!" she hissed.

Penny gloated too. "She *loved* the pie I made. Bought a whole pie *and* tipped us one hundred dollars." Penny snapped the green bill.

Liam chuckled and instructed Penny to hide the cash away from the boys who just might want to take her credit. After all, the Prairie Creek High pie table was the talk of the entire event, he informed them.

"Speaking of which, there's someone here to talk to you." Liam gently cupped Molly's elbow and turned her toward the hangar doors.

Mr. Porter, with Betsy at his side, stood, hands clasped behind his back, whistling and wandering directly toward Molly and Liam.

Molly grabbed Liam's hand. "Don't leave me. Please."

He squeezed her hand back. "I'm not going anywhere." She shot him a quick, grateful smile, then turned her attention to Mr. Porter.

"Hello, Ms. Maison," he boomed merrily.

"Hi, Mr. Porter. And Merry Christmas!" She held up a piece of Parker Porter's pecan pie. "Your son made this."

Mr. Porter took the plate and the fork she offered and dove in without hesitation. He came up grinning, mouth full, and mumbled through the dessert, "This is the best pie I've ever had! Where is that boy?"

Liam answered, "I sent him and Dwayne into town to pick up Mrs. Zick and drive her here."

"Mr. Porter, about my contract," Molly wasn't afraid to

launch right into her request. Namely, that she get back at least one Culinary Arts class for starters. She'd do whatever else they needed of her, if they could at least give her just *one* class.

"Oh, Ms. Maison. I hope you'll forgive us. And when I say *us* I mean the entire school board. There's a bit of tunnel vision among the members, and it took a wake-up call for us to realize that we had something even more valuable."

"Liam's threat to pull the ranch?" she asked, unable to withhold the smugness that clouded her voice.

Mr. Porter's eyes widened, though. "Pull the ranch?" He looked at Liam. "What?"

Confused, Molly interjected, "That's why you're talking to me, right? Because your only cooperating ranch is closing its doors." She looked from Mr. Porter to Liam and back again.

Liam's face was unreadable, but Mr. Porter shook his head heavily, and his face reddened. "Liam, I can't believe you're going to do that."

Molly also looked at Liam. "Wait, I thought you were going to tell him..."

"I didn't need to, Molly. When Betsy went to the board Monday night, ready to fight for you, she was met with a whole ensemble of people who beat her to the punch."

"What are you talking about?" Molly felt the rug being tugged from beneath her feet, but instead of falling, she was floating.

"That's right, Ms. Maison. Monday night's emergency school board meeting had a call to the public from the likes of your students, including Penny and Porter, Dwayne, and others, as well as their parents and, the loudest voice among them all, Mrs. Zick. I didn't realize the woman knew what a school board was. She comes from a one-room schoolhouse, I'm fairly sure." He guffawed until he was wheezing, and while Molly floated there, speechless, Liam went on.

"Molly, they rallied behind you, arguing that the ag program was great but the culinary program was better."

"If you'll stay, Ms. Maison, we'd like to sign you on for a full-time contract beginning in January."

"No agriculture? But that was the lifeblood, I thought. Everyone in this town wants ag."

"You're right," Mr. Porter confirmed. "But I have one teacher for such an extracurricular program, and that's you. And what you do best is cook and teach kids how to cook. Shame on me for ever greenlighting the board's discussion on opening up that can of beans."

"Oh, it's...it's okay."

"No, it's not. But it will be, because not only that, but your program will also be fully funded, isn't that right, Phil?" Liam pressed.

"Are you serious?" Molly felt her entire body go weightless, like she might drift off on a snowflake across the prairie. "Fully funded? Full-time position?"

"Everything. All of it."

"And no agriculture program, though?"

"Unless we can find someone to take over, no. It'll take a backseat, for now." He then eyed Liam. "Unless..."

Molly lit up from within. Of course! It was *obvious*. "Liam," she said, her feet back on the ground and her heart racing with anticipation. "You could teach. You could teach the ag program."

Liam looked thoughtfully at her, then at Mr. Porter. "It's an idea."

"It's a great one, if I do say so myself!" He clapped Liam on the shoulder and said, "Son, let's talk after the weekend, all right? We could pare it down, even." He held his hands out like he was framing his words. "Something-something *Homesteading for High Schoolers*. How about that?"

Liam answered dreamily, "Sure. Okay."

Then, Mr. Porter turned once more to Molly. "Ms. Maison, I've made a mess of this whole situation, and for that, I'm truly sorry. I'm sorry it took a gang of your supporters to bring me to my senses. I'm sorry I wasted all this time."

As her principal was apologizing, pearls of wisdom crept up into Molly's mind. Something her mimi had once told her. *Even if you have all the right ingredients and you follow the recipe, things can turn out much differently than you wanted. This, Molly Maison, is not a waste.*

"It wasn't a waste of time, Mr. Porter." But as she said it, he was finishing his pie and someone from another booth was calling him and Betsy over to them, and soon enough it was just Liam and Molly again.

"If it wasn't a waste of time, then what was it?" Liam asked her, lacing his hands through hers in full display of their students and Creek folk. His words were playful, and so was Molly's response. Behind them, a photo booth was set up for selfies and quick pictures. It was Christmas themed with a real live spruce tree, ornaments, lights, and a pergola at the top of which hung a pretty bough of mistletoe. She pulled Liam beneath the bough and tugged his face down to hers, kissing him before she replied at last.

"A delicious mess."

He kissed her once again, and when they came up for air, Liam asked, "By the way, what was that secret of yours?"

"Secret?" She thought back to their conversations, shuffling through all the kissing and hand holding, hugging, and flirting. "Oh. Right."

"You were falling for me. That's what it was, right? You were into me from the moment you laid eyes on me, huh?"

Molly pursed her lips impishly and shook her head. "That was one of them, yes."

"There's another?" He rolled their interlocked hands down to their sides, slid his hands from hers and wrapped her up in a hug, their hips pressed together. "If you have another secret, I have to know what it is. Let me guess. You put a spell on me with that peanut butter sandwich. I knew it. I knew it tasted too good to be true."

"It's not exactly a secret, actually," she answered. "It's a truth. One of three truths in cooking that Mimi taught me."

"What's this truth then?"

"She always told me that if you cook from here—" Molly tapped a finger on her chest and looked up into his eyes, where Molly could see that Mimi had been right. "If you cook from your *heart*, then your food is love."

* * *

If you enjoyed this story, don't miss the next book in Prairie Creek: *A Prairie Creek Christmas*.

Also by Elizabeth Bromke

Prairie Creek:

The Country Cottage

The Thimble Shoppe

A Homestead Holiday

A Prairie Creek Christmas

Other Series

Heirloom Island

Harbor Hills

Birch Harbor

Hickory Grove

Gull's Landing

Maplewood

About the Author

Elizabeth Bromke writes women's fiction and contemporary romance. She lives in the mountains of northern Arizona with her husband, son, and their sweet dogs, Winnie and Tuesday. After teaching secondary English for thirteen lucky years, she stopped teaching about stories and started writing them.

Learn more about the author by visiting her website at elizabethbromke.com.

Acknowledgments

As always, a great big thanks to my wonderful editor, Lisa Lee. Thank you, Lisa, for being a great friend and for having a great eye! Marge Burke, thank you so much for your support and friendship and keen eye, as well. And thank you to Joy Lorton for your very careful work on proofreading this manuscript. I'm so glad to have connected with you!

Wilette Cruz: thank you for drawing readers in with your stunning cover design.

Always a great big thanks to my wonderful family, who stick by my side through it all.

Never last or least, my two Eddies, I love you! Thank you for being my reason!

Made in the USA
Middletown, DE
18 November 2022

15377166R00123